Someone To Crawl Back To

Published by **Boson Books**
Raleigh, NC 27606
ISBN 1-886420-98-X

An imprint of **C&M Online Media Inc.**

"Dance Party" first appeared in *The Chattahoochee Review*,
Volume XI, Number 4, Summer 1991, pp. 60-65

"Murmurs" first appeared in *Gulf Stream Magazine*,
Volume 9, 1994, pp. 35-48

"Sunspots," a South Carolina Fiction Project winner, first
appeared in *The State* Newspaper, October 27, 1991, pp. 19-20

"Wrecker," a South Carolina Fiction Project winner, first appeared
in *The Post and Courier* Newspaper, July 16, 2000, pp. 1-2H

"Vibes" is a Piccolo Spoleto Fiction 2000 award recipient

Cover photo by Rick Cary
Cover design by Once Removed

C&M Online Media Inc.
www.cmonline.com
boson@cmonline.com

To Nancy McAllister

Someone

To

Crawl Back

To

Phillip Gardner

Boson Books   Raleigh

Contents

Prologue
Talk
Rene Severance

There are some conversations you can't have. To have them is to ruin everything. Either/Or conversations are one example. There is no such thing as an Either/Or conversation. There are only OR conversations.

There are others you can't have. If you have them everything is over. And if everything is over you die inside. Not all at once, but you die; it's a sure thing.

There are conversations you have to have, no matter what. Because you *must* have them, they usually end in a matterless world of talk. There are things you have to say because if you don't say them you have no chance of stopping the thing that has to be stopped–before it does damage that can't be undone. These are all conversations you must have.

You can't have conversations about lost passion. Passion is a thing that can only be discussed when it is present. If you have it, or if two people share it, they can spend hours in delicious conversation. This is the nature of passion. To talk about the absence of passion is to ruin any chance of regaining it, to doom it to purgatory. Of course the only reason to have that conversation is in order somehow to save it. There is nothing to be gained and everything to be lost. Maybe not to talk about it is to keep it alive, or to keep alive the chance that it may return. Some people who are clinically dead come back.

Words can do almost anything, repair almost any pain. But they can do nothing for lost passion. So it is pointless to have a conversation about it. The person who no longer possesses that feeling can't be held responsible, not really. Nobody chooses to give up those feelings. Nobody is to blame, not really. Sometimes people get tired or distracted, sometimes they get lonely, sometimes they are mysteriously attracted to other lovers. It's not a thing they choose. If they *could* go on feeling that feeling with someone, they would. It's not a thing to blame someone for, the loss of passion I mean. It's not a thing people choose. So there is really no reason to think that talking will do any good.

If she says, *I have lost the feeling for you*, what can he say? He can't restore good feelings by making her feel bad, guilty for something that isn't her fault. That would eliminate all possibility for restoring the thing he most wants to save. You don't want to do that. That would be cruel, because even as he said, *Please love me* he would be making it all impossible. Sometimes it makes you want to cry, but that does no good; that is a conversation with yourself and does nothing to restore the passion that, in its absence, makes you want to cry.

So if you love somebody, it is essential to say the things you have to say and to avoid the things you must never say.

Chain of Fools
Joshua Severance and John D. Truett

I drink decaffeinated coffee in the morning and lite beer at night. I drink a lot of both. The coffee gives the illusion of morning, of things getting off to a start. The beer gives the day closure. It takes a while, but it gets closed, eventually. What happens in between is what I'm trying to get in order, so I divide the day as evenly as I can between the decaf and the lite. It's one way of establishing balance. Balance is the important thing.

When other disillusioned people see that you're working at working things out, it makes them nervous. If you're depressed all the time, have predictable psychotic fits, or drink too much and play air guitar on the bar at the Paradise Lounge, people get used to that. But once they sense that you're seriously trying to figure things out, you become the horse that shits in their parade. Just ask F. Scott Fitzgerald. Or my ex-shrink.

"Earlier, you referred to your marriage as an 'expired lot.' You said, 'Ours is the story of two people who met and fell in love. Then one of us fell out of love.'" This was my shrink speaking. "I think there is serious meaning in 'expired lot,' Josh."

"Look," I said, "I sell pharmaceuticals for a living. It's language of the trade. If I were a carburetor man or a proctologist, I suppose I'd find another metaphor."

But my shrink, Something Pratt, wouldn't buy it. Poor guy had the look of a human punching bag.

The therapy was killing me. So, step one, I dumped my therapist. And I felt better–like finally parking your car after a long trip of competing for the wheel. At seventy-five dollars a pop, I figured I could clean the counter of decaf and the cooler of Milwaukee's Best Lite for the price of one session. Besides, Mr. Pratt had developed a pattern of starting each session with personal experiences that began, "When *I* first entered therapy–." I suppose he wanted me to seize upon a single word, make him angry, work him through his anger, and then leave him with the illusion of having found some balance. I had better things to do. Like drinking with my attorney.

My friend John Truett and I were driving into town to get away from our wives. I'd lost the only one I'd ever wanted, and he couldn't leave the one he had. We never talked directly about our fractured interior lives, but I could see the scars and so could he. Neither of us was in a very talkative mood. We passed a building with a big dish out front, a church. The year before it had been a VFW bar.

"That wrestling joint is a church now," I said, craning my neck as we passed. We'd gone to a women's wrestling event there some time back. One of the women wrestlers had singled out John to rub baby oil all over her. It's part of the act. I knew he'd remember. I hoped it would lift his spirits.

"That was the day of O. J.'s famous Bronco drive," he said. John is my lawyer. He remembers those sorts of things. He's good at making connections between unlikely possibilities. One day maybe he'll be rich. Divorce is big business.

That afternoon John had learned that his wife was pregnant for the sixth time. In law school he'd fallen in love with her milk makers—she had enormous breasts—and she hadn't had a dry day in ten years. Their capacity seemed inexhaustible.

As his family had grown, John the man had seemed to shrink proportionately, his appearance more starched, his mind more pressed. It took some doing, and several whiskeys, to get his sense of humor pried away from his too tightly knotted necktie. Once he got going, though, he was funnier than anyone I knew.

"What did Adam say to Eve in the Garden of Eden?" I asked. He grinned. "Stand back, Eve, I don't know *how* big this thing is gonna get."

We laughed. "That's Robin Williams," I said. We laughed some more. John kept laughing until his eyes were all watery. Still he kept laughing. I wanted to change the subject. I thought hard, hoping to tell him another one, but my mind went blank. He tried to hold his breath to stop the little lurches in his shoulders. He didn't look at me. We drove some more.

"I've got a truth for you, Josh," John said. We had been sitting for a while at the bar in the Paradise Lounge talking movies. John was still in lawyer mode. Contemporary films, he'd argued, don't tell the truth about the ways ordinary men are sometimes defeated in marital relations. John's theory is that women can find complete satisfaction through childbearing, but men, once they've done their part, have no equivalent. And since the man's function is instinctively not monogamous, the theory goes, men live as slaves to a domestic order defined by women, a fact never confronted by men or women in our culture. For men to admit to domestic slavery would, by definition, make them less than men, John says. So long as women can portray themselves as victims and convince men that they are the victimizers, women hold the upper hand. They own the cultural guilt factor, their big stick, so to speak. I wasn't sure I wanted to hear John's truth.

"Maternity is invested with an arsenal of prerogatives," he said. "I see it in court every day. I use it like a machete in divorce cases."

I said that men could create art. John passed about four ounces of beer through his nose.

George Miles, the bartender, brought us another one. He saw the look on John's face. "This rounds on me, Bo," George said softly, looking from John to me. He moved down the bar, outside the range of the conversation, then glanced back.

"You said you had a truth," I said. "I hope it's a new one." John lifted his sunglasses from his pocket, turned and looked at me through the black lenses.

"You never know how big a woman's ass is until you start to kiss it." His face was impassive behind the dark circles of glass. "Truth. Take it from me. I should know, I've been there. When it comes to gluteus maximus geography, I've been to Montana and back." He lifted his drink in a toast. "Drink up," he said. "Let's get out of here."

"You drive," John said in the parking lot outside the Paradise Lounge. "If you get caught, I'll represent you for free. If I get caught, I'll have to pay."

"Okay," I said. "Give me the keys."

"No way," he said. "You're a threat to every woman and child on the highway."

"No," I said. "Only to every woman."

"On the highway? You kinky bastard."

I sang a song off The Beatles' *White Album*, and we laughed. Then a kind of heavy silence filled the car, and I got that bad, empty feeling about things.

At the intersection of Laurel and Providence Road, the light turned, and we stopped behind a van. John read aloud the lettering on the back, "Terminex." He opened the door and walked up to the driver, whose face I could see in his side mirror. I couldn't hear what John was saying. The guy smiled. Then his face went absolutely blank, as if someone had pulled the plug. His window started up, but John held his hand on it. John said something else. I would have sworn he was asking directions or something. Then the guy must have cranked hard on the handle, because the window zipped up. John took out his wallet and showed him some money. Then he held his hands together, thumbs up, as if he were playing imaginary saxophone or something, only he was inhaling, drawing hard on the imaginary pipe or whatever. John doesn't play the saxophone.

Anyway, the guy ran the light just before it turned green. John shrugged and started back toward me in the headlights. By the time he got behind the wheel, horns were blowing. The engine was running. He gently shifted the transmission into drive.

"I should have gone into medicine," he said. Then he didn't say anything for a while. "I should have gone into medicine like my brother."

"They make a bundle."

"True," he said. "My brother has two houses and three wives. Two of them are ex-wives. Drives a Jag. Happiest man I know."

"Big mistake on your part," I said. "What does he do?"

"Hearts maybe. No, no it's lungs. He quit smoking after he did his first set of lungs. When you see what's inside, well, you know." He was drifting. "I could *quit* smoking."

I knew what he meant. He'd seen people rip each other's hearts out, had been a paid accomplice.

"What's new in divorce court?" I said. Sometimes he dealt with it by focusing on the absurdity of his work. He was drunk enough now. If he got started, I knew he'd run with it. He could remember whole dialogues, exchanges between soon-to-be ex-spouses. Some of them were as funny as anything you can imagine. But he didn't seem to hear me.

"I could *stop* smoking," he said.

One wing on the blue-and-red neon sign outside Byrd's poolroom was broken. When the other wing blinked up and down, it created the impression of a diving left turn. We parked the car in a space where somebody, some kid I guess, had left his letter jacket—a blue one with red sleeves. It was flat with tire tracks. We were singing harmony by this time to the radio. We are both pretty good singers. Really.

Byrd, the owner, is fond of John, too. John represented Byrd during his divorce. For months, every time John walked in, Byrd would cup his balls and say to some customer sitting across the bar or to his second wife, "See that guy? He's the reason I still got these." For months Byrd gave him free drinks. He greeted us with a warm, vigorous handshake.

John and I leaned against the bar and waited for our beers. Nothing inside Byrd's poolroom had changed in twenty years, maybe longer. It's the sort of place that has been around since the beginning of time. Byrd could have bought new tables or made a killing on video games and poker machines, but the tables never changed, except that he had them railed and covered when they became untrue. His regulars know those tables. John and I were regulars.

Even the records on the jukebox hadn't changed. Most were rhythm and blues numbers: "I've Been Loving You Too Long," by Otis Redding; "Mustang Sally," by Wilson Pickett; Percy Sledge's, "When a Man Loves a Woman." Songs like that. "Chain of Fools" was playing now.

The lights were dim, except for the fluorescent tents above each of the ten tables that stretched the length of the narrow brick room. Steps led down to the level of the tables, and if you wanted, you could sit at the bar and follow any game below. The green felt colors soothed my eyes. And the pleasant combination of waxed hardwood floors, beer, hot-dog chili, and baby powder gave my brain a rest.

But the place had the opposite effect on John. He was suddenly alive. Lifting his arms, wrists cuffed above his bowed head, he strutted toward the bar singing with the Queen of Soul. Byrd smiled at him from behind the bar, pulled out two more Budweisers, and wrung the caps off. Evander Baker and Joe Fales, who were at the third table, lifted their sticks and started chanting, "John-ny, John-ny." The others took it up. Whenever any of those guys got locked up, day or night, or split with their wives or got split from them, they called John. I stepped over to the bar to pay for the beers, and John went into a version of "the swim," his head bobbing to Aretha Franklin, gliding down the steps, past the tables, giving high-fives to everyone.

"Happy Hour for you guys all night," Byrd said, leaning in confidentially.

John was singing louder now as the song reached the vamp, and all the players had stopped shooting and were smiling. Most were singing with him, singing the chorus of "Chain of Fools." Byrd wagged his head from side to side, wiping the bar with a white rag with a red border. "He's crazy," Byrd said. "He's crazy."

Time passed into no time. Somebody had been buying fireballs, a red cinnamon drink, and splitting them two or three ways. But now it was tequila shots we were drinking. Byrd and John were doing bar tricks for the less serious players and those who'd lost their money. Byrd walked the length of the bar with a spoon on his nose, and John dropped lighted matches into two shot glasses in front of him on the bar.

Joe Fales was telling a story I'd heard before about how he'd set some guy's face on fire in chemistry class, then rushed him to the bathroom and dunked his head in the toilet. It was his example of having saved somebody's life.

John pressed a shot glass against each side of his neck. The matches died, forming a vacuum, and the glasses stuck. He stood slowly, then, darting his head like a rooster to the music, danced across the floor, to a song called "Skinny Legs and All."

Byrd took out a toothpick, bent it in two, then bent each like knees.

"Come here, John," Byrd called above the music. "I'll show you how to get a woman to spread her legs." John swayed over. Byrd licked the original break in the toothpick and the wooden knees sprang up.

"I got one for you," said Joe Fales.

John slowly pulled the shot glasses from each side of his neck and turned his back to the bar. Two raised red islands remained. "You gonna have some explaining to do when the ole Lady sees those," said Evander. "If that ain't a hell of a hickey, I'll kiss your ass." Joe was laying out rows of peanuts on the bar.

John pushed away from the bar, then drifted down the steps and swayed unsteadily past tables where the money was getting serious, on back to the last table, the only empty one. He picked up a stick and began banking the cue, hitting it so hard it ricocheted off the rails.

Joe Fales traced circles on a napkin with a pencil and a quarter, then put the napkin in front of Evander on the bar. "Roll the quarter down your nose, and if it lands touching any one of the circles, I'll buy you a drink." Evander pressed the coin between his eyes and rolled it the length of his beak. Each time, a new lead pencil line ran down his nose. Everybody was laughing, laughing at Evander who was laughing at them. Then we heard John.

He was standing in the center of the last table with his pool cue-turned-microphone singing "My Way." Everybody laughed. "Get off my table, you dumbshit." Byrd was laughing too. John kept singing, going down on one knee like a crooner. He didn't stop singing. The laughing stopped. Eyes turned to Byrd.

"Time to go," I said to John, who had begun the first verse again. "Come on man, get down from there. I'll buy you a drink, then we'll go."

"Can't make me."

He jumped to the next table, where Harman Parnell, the mobile home guy, and a one-eyed man I didn't know were playing. The balls went everywhere. He slipped and fell hard on the green felt-covered slate. It was Harman's money on the game.

"Hey, asshole."

John took out his wallet, emptied it on the table. "Next game's on me."

Byrd, Joe, and Evander were coming down the steps. The place was otherwise frozen.

John pushed himself up again, stepped toward the rail. "I will now perform a half-gainer into the side pocket."

"Get down," I said.

"Otherwise known as a belly flop."

At the next table, Mitchell Watford stood in front of him, cue stick raised.

"Take out your score cards, gentlemen." He dove onto the next table, going down hard, landing on his side. His mouth was bleeding. Mitchell grabbed him by the shirt, but I pushed him away. Byrd and I helped John down.

He found his footing, stretched his arms, threw back his head. He really was bleeding. "I did it Myyyyyyyyyyy way." Then he gave a deep, theatrical bow. Nobody was laughing.

He went into a three-point stance like a running back and darted the length of the room, dodging players, up the steps, disappearing behind the bar. I picked up his wallet and began stuffing his money inside it when I felt a hand on my shoulder. I looked up expecting trouble, but it was Evander Baker, looking away, at the other end of the pool hall, at John, who was standing alone on the bar with Byrd's revolver at his head.

"This is the audience participation part of the show," he said. He wiped the blood from his mouth. "I'm gonna do this bar trick I saw once." He took a deep breath. "Everybaaa-dy having a good time? Then, let me hear you say *hell* yeah." He cupped his hand at his ear. The room was absolutely still. You could hear the slow turning of the ceiling fans. "Dead crowd," he said. "Blame it on the opening act."

I started toward the bar. "Put the goddamn gun down, John."

"You are in charge of crowd control, Josh," he said, motioning for me to stop. "Now, I'm gonna show you the best fuckin' bar trick you ever saw. Are you read-eeee? But I need your help."

He moved slowly down the bar toward us. "You see, I'll blow my brains out, here, live-and-in-person, like you ain't *never* seen, if you guys will just promise to take care of my wife and kids, okay? Like in the Old South, in the old days, a casualty of war. What do you say? I know I can count on you. Let's see a little commitment here." It was hard to look at him. Some men leaned on their sticks and looked down at the floor.

"Let's have a show of hands. Come on, how much is that asking?" With his free hand, he shook an imaginary pompom. "You-can-do-it, you-can-do-it, you can." He took another deep breath. "Come on guys, it's my wife and kids" he pleaded. "Just make sure nobody fucks with them, that's all I'm asking. I'd do it for any one of your fuckers, wouldn't I?" I was the only one looking at him. "You fuckers."

"Come on, John."

"Let me buy you a drink, man."

"Call it a day, Pal."

"Hand me the gun, brother," I said. We all waited, looking but trying not to look, afraid.

John lowered the pistol, then sat with his legs dangling from the bar. "How much is that asking? I'd do as much for any man in this room." He looked from one down-turned face to another. He still held the gun. "You're all a bunch of pussies. You're all pussies."

For the first time, I think, he realized he was bleeding. He wiped his mouth, then eased himself down and walked to the jukebox, the pistol hanging loosely at his side. Nobody moved. Nobody spoke. He dropped two quarters into the machine, set the revolver on the glass, and pressed the numbers. He hovered over it, its lights hollowing his eyes, illuminating his rising and contracting chest.

A saxophone suddenly blasted, the brick walls boosting the volume it seemed Jr. Walker and the All-Stars: "Shotgun." The record skipped with a dtic, dtic between the lyrics. John gave the corner of the machine a cushioned blow with the palm of his hand. Then again. His head plumed up in anger. Gripping the edges of the machine, he rocked it gently.

Then his body exploded in electrocution-like surges.

The needle screamed off the vinyl. John stopped. And we listened to the slow, predictable mechanical whine of the player's arm rejecting, then coming to rest.

I laid my hand on his shoulder.

It was so cold I had the heater blowing full blast, but John had his window down.

"Pull in here," he said.

"Too late to buy beer now."

"Pull in. I want cigarettes."

The fluorescent lights inside the WILL-MART convenience store were as bright as lights in an operating room, so bright I could see his reflection in the cooler door. The reflection did something to his face. He circled back toward the counter.

The woman cashier sat on a tall wooden stool watching a tiny TV screen. When she stood, she curled one arm under her bowling ball-sized belly and slid sideways to her feet. John said something and she looked down, smiling at her stomach, then suddenly looked up at him as if he were a ghost. I reached for the door handle. She looked terrified. The pregnant woman quickly handed over the cigarettes, avoiding his eyes. I pushed the door open. John just stood there looking down at her, then turned and started back out to the car.

I don't know why, but I turned on the blinker in the parking lot before pulling out onto the street. John was tearing the cellophane off the Lucky Strikes. As far as I knew he had never smoked.

"What did you say to her?" I asked.

"Asked if she loved her baby." He pulled the lighter from the dash and lit up.

"What did she say?"

He puffed. "That she did." He pressed a button, and his window went up in silence. "So I asked her why she ate him." He bumped a second cigarette from the pack and lit it from the first, then offered it to me.

"No thanks."

He tucked the filter of each cigarette under his top lip so that they looked like red-tipped fangs. The smoke streamed up his cheeks, over his eyes, through his hair.

Then he stared straight ahead, his eyes fixed on some image in the glass or beyond it or on nothing at all farther away.

Ahead, the road seemed to meet me, as if it were being created the moment the headlights touched it, and I took the curves slowly, concentrating on the very center of the lane, focusing, feeling the comfort of that concentration.

John began singing "Smoke Gets In Your Eyes," a little slower than the original, but at near perfect pitch.

After a time, I joined in.

You find balance in small things. For example, think about how hot you like your coffee and about how cool it gets before you don't want it anymore. About how cold you want your beer and how slowly you can drink it before it becomes an obligation. I know, these are small things. But try it. You have to start with the balance of small things. It takes some time, but try it. Then over time and if you're lucky, maybe you find the perfect balance in your day between the coffee and the beer. Then move to the bigger things. Maybe it can make a remarkable difference.

Inhabited Space
Giles Carter

After two sober weeks of sitting all day in the sun writing, Giles did produce a scenario finally, a good one he thought. And so in the end it turned out all right, or at least that's what he told himself.

But that first day Giles lay in bed well into the afternoon, thinking of the drive from the airport to the hotel. Nobody in the limo said the screenplay wouldn't work and would have to be scrapped. Nobody said it. But everybody knew.

Giles reached for another cigarette on the table beside the bed, lit it, and began to replay yet again the drive to the Hilton from LA International, feeling only the oscillation of panic and awe. The scene inside the stretch Lincoln had played so smoothly, unfolding seamlessly, every inflection perfect, every pause charged with silent meaning. If he could just remember how it had really happened, he might be able to use it sometime. He had lost so much because he'd forgotten how things had really been.

Now all he could recall truly was the blood rushing through his ears and an internal voice saying, Something is wrong here; something is very, very wrong. He couldn't remember a single line of dialogue from the thirty-minute drive. He had lost it.

When he finally got dressed Giles was still on East Coast time, and he went for a walk in the stark sunlight because his internal clock said it was time for a drink. He had the small blue notebook, which he carried in his pocket to remind himself that it didn't necessarily have to be a lie, his saying he was a writer.

The next day, after Giles had searched until he'd found the bar again, the barman, a Swede, refused to return the little notebook. "I'm gonna fuck up your world, Bubba," Giles had said with such conviction that the Swede, who had thirty pounds on him, reached for the phone and called the police.

But that first day, the blonde had taken the notebook from Giles's pocket and laid it before him, then opened the button on his shirt and pressed her fingers on his nipple. Later, he vaguely remembered, there had been some shouting from the Swede about the bill.

The bar, The Booth it was named, was narrow and dark, a neighborhood geriatric bar in North Hollywood. People knew one another. They were all very, very old. Somebody spoke when someone new walked in. Giles Carter sat among them and listened for conversation that he might use in a script sometime. Rhett Butler's stand-in arrived, the ears and mustache perfectly preserved, the ancient, tanned face a wrinkled mask. The old man had traded on that role, Giles thought, that moment, all these years, playing the refracted part of a man pretending to be Clark Gable acting the part of Rhett Butler, a fiction.

After his first novel, Giles had promoted himself like a brush salesman. He'd thought the promotional persona would force him to get the second book written. If he went public enough about the second book, he'd have to write it. If he were bold enough it would be a good book. He'd have to hold true to it. That's what he had thought at the time.

"What about Hollywood?" the interviewer from *Publishers Weekly* had asked.

"Hollywood is a whore in a wedding dress," he'd said.

That was before he had signed the contract to write the screenplay that wouldn't work.

Sitting alone at a small table inside The Booth, he drank and soaked in the dark coolness, then drank more. And sometime later when there was still light outside, two women came in and took a small table behind him. Giles watched them in the mirror above the bar and listened. One was tall and blonde, mini-skirted and well built, English. The other, brownish-red haired and weathered, said she was from Colorado. He thought she looked made of desert material. He sat so that he could listen like a secret agent. Both women had played hooky from work, the tall, good-looking one because her Colorado friend had just been broken off from a relationship. They drank. The English blonde pressed buttons on the jukebox. Heads turned.

Later, much later, an old woman, one of the regulars, came into the bar with her wares and set up shop on the tiny area that had been meant for a bandstand and sold—what? And Giles thought, yes, Fellini.

"Your accent, is it real?" the blonde said.

Giles was standing at a telephone, music behind him, without the number he thought he'd intended to call.

"I have my hand on your leg," she said after other drinks.

He awaited the hole he was going to make in the windshield on the drive over, and they parked in an alley that made him think danger. Then he was looking around for a bed.

He thought it would go quickly. Even the earth's axis seemed to him greased, all things gliding now, the city a pastel patched quilt easing around him. But instead they were standing in the apartment kitchen, small and narrow and empty, and someone, a man, arrived and then wasn't there.

A NEW VOICE: "You didn't go to work. You should have told me, you know. When you didn't show for dinner, I called the office. I gave you away." The tanned, athletic girl who was talking to the tall blonde woman he was with hadn't taken her eyes off him since appearing from vapor just now. Her eyes never left Giles.

The girl was young, maybe sixteen, if you didn't count the eyes. Giles didn't know what to say. Why was she telling *him* this? Dinner? Whose office? She waited for his reply. Now a reversal: she looked at her mother but spoke to him. "I have my license, but hers is a five-speed. What's your name?" she said, still looking at her mother. Then he realized she was still talking to him.

"Giles Carter," he said.

"Giiiles," she repeated. "What does it mean?"

Then the girl was gone, and Giles and the girl's mother were drinking vodka. "She approves of you," the woman said. "She likes you. Couldn't you tell by the way she was looking at you?"

"But I'm not from Mississippi. You told her I was from Mississippi. South Carolina. I'm from South Carolina."

"She likes you. She likes the way you are."

He sits on the sofa with a photo album on his lap. There is no other furniture in the room. The snapshots seem familiar. Has he seen the people in the photos before? He half expects to see himself on the next page. But what the girl says about each picture is unfamiliar, the connections between one picture and another just beyond his reach. The woman in the kitchen making more vodkas is smiling from inside the picture her daughter points at. Giles forgets where he is.

When she reaches the last page, the girl tilts up the photo album and the pages flip backwards like celluloid squares, rewinding time, reconstructing the narrative: Boy gets Girl, Boy loses Girl, Boy meets Girl.

Giles sees two sofas, like an L here. One mattress on the floor framed by the bedroom door there. That is all. Where does the music come from?

The girl looks up at him and smiles brightly.

He decides. No sleeping with the tall one he drove over with, no going to bed with all those photos creating disturbing scenes, all that history to carry in his head. Even drunk, he feels the levitating sensation of having decided and knowing that no amount of drink can change his mind about this one.

After a few seconds, he realizes the girl's mother is talking to him. "I've promised a driving lesson, you understand. You won't go away, will you?" she says. "Promise? Won't be long."

Her daughter waits impatiently at the door, observing. "The girl sees wax figures through thick glass," Giles whispers.

"Promise that you won't sleep with her," the English mother says, looking past him, speaking now of the brownish-red haired Colorado friend who has been broken off of a relationship–who has been in the apartment somewhere all along.

"No, I won't."

The daughter stands holding the door, looking at him. She doesn't extend her hand to protect her mother as the woman weaves past her. The girl is still looking at him after the mother has negotiated the landing, still looking at him. The mother is on the stairs now, and Giles thinks she'll never make it down in one piece.

"We'll be back, but you won't be here. So I'll say good-bye," the girl said.

"I'll be here."

"Sure you will." She turned, then looked back. "But I like the sound of your voice when you say that." He heard her running down the steps before the door closed behind her. He heard a voice. Then he was inside his own head.

INTERIOR - APARTMENT - NIGHT

That brown-red color, like Colorado, was fine. Just right really. But from the view Giles had now, CLOSE UP, the roots should have been black, or better yet blonde. She should have had it dyed. All wrong not to have had it dyed. He was sure she should have. No question. The Colorado Woman. Her breasts sway in the water.

WOMAN

Let's take a bath.

Turning her face up to us now, toward the camera, toward him; the camera is at EYE LEVEL. He steps back, out of the frame.

THE GIRL
(voice
over)
The woman who calls herself my mother
wants her purse. You got it?

CUT TO:

WOMAN
Must've left it at the bar.

CUT TO:

THE GIRL
(hip against the
sink but leaning in
as she speaks)
Well *THESE* keys are mine and I
won't be handing them over.

CUT TO: CLOSE UP

For a second the keys between her thumb and first knuckle flap like a small fish grasped by its head.

CUT TO:

THE GIRL as she opens the WOMAN'S BAG, lights a cigarette from it, blows out the smoke, watches as the smoke finally disappears. Then looks again at the WOMAN in the bath. A long moment here.

THE GIRL
You don't waste much time, do you?

She pulls hard on the cigarette and allows the smoke to float from her lips, sizes up the naked woman in the bath and the fully dressed man standing above her.

FADE TO BLACK

He liked the girl very much now, the way she walked into the scene, delivered her lines, took control of the whole thing, powerful in the spaces between the words, the calculated pauses, rhetorical silence.
"I'd like to stick around, you know, just to watch. Just to watch, you understand, but Mummy might get *SUSPICIOUS*, and then I would never learn to drive."

It seemed to Giles that the phone rang before the girl could have possibly gotten downstairs to the Volkswagen. The woman with the brown-red hair who was wearing only a towel held the phone at arm's length, tears in her eyes, her face still swollen from crying.
"No, I didn't," he replied into the receiver. "No, I didn't."
Unlike early gray L.A. mornings, mornings that always promised rain and would have meant rain anywhere else but burned away instead— or L.A.'s cool evening breeze that in South Carolina could only have meant spring dawn, L.A. darkness was like darkness everywhere else.
"She was too drunk for *ME* to drive," the girl said, charging across the room to the sofa.
"Was not." The tall, blonde mother smiled, pushed back the cloud of fine hair from the girl's sulky eyes.
"I thought you might pass out and I would drive us up to Tehachapi. You're a born human sacrifice, you know." She turned her eyes up to Giles now and smiled. "Some day she's gonna wake up with a knife in her heart." She kissed her mother's cheek.
"She's such a very pretty girl. So beautiful I pity her," the mother said.

"Pity is as pity does."

"Just turned sixteen." Together she and Giles watched the girl disappear into the room with only a mattress on the floor. "I was that beautiful."

She poured vodkas into tall glasses. But he didn't drink.

The four of them sat on the L-shaped sofa inside a long, empty silence. "Oh, gross," the girl said. She looked at her mother and they both laughed. The Colorado woman in the towel had passed out with her legs apart. The girl went to her, looked at the Giles, lifted the towel, raised her eyebrows high like Groucho Marx.

"Let's shave her a valentine," the girl said to him.

"That would be painful and cruel."

"Yes, so what are you saying?"

His glass of clear, warm vodka sat on the floor.

"Time for little girls to be beddy-bye."

The girl made a face that could only be made in the presence of the blind.

"But why, Mommy? You are much too drunk to fuck."

"Bed. Now . . . . Young Lady?"

"Much too drunk to *be* fucked, I might add."

The girl closed the door of the room with only a mattress. She didn't look back.

When they danced, he realized the mother was exactly his height, eyes and lips spaced the same. He led her back to the sofa to sleep. Giles backed away from her, toward the source of the music. Dim yellow light reflected off the narrow kitchen walls and fell like sulfurous smoke over the two sleeping women.

Behind the curtain he found the radio. It was the only life left in the room. Leaning forward into the bay window, forearms on the sill, Giles experienced the sensation of standing at the stern of a giant ship, a deep cold current just beneath his feet. He didn't know how far it was back to the bar, distance being measured in space and time, with two of the three parts of the equation having been suspended indefinitely. But he figured he'd be sober by the time he got back to where he remembered things clearly.

When he knocked on the bedroom door there was no answer, but he could see the light from inside. He eased open the door. The girl looked up from her magazine.

"Can you tell me how to get back to the bar? Do you know which one?"

"It's The Booth. Tell the taxi man. They all know it." She returned to her reading.

"I'll be walking."

"It's too far," she said without looking up. She lifted the edge of the mattress. "Here. This will get you there."

"No."

"It's okay. I'll tell her she spent it on drink. Half true, huh? The way I see it, it's you who deserves it, even if you didn't earn it."

"I really couldn't do that."

"You are funny. Talk to me and I'll see to it that you get home safe."

"I'm sorry?"

"Just talk to me. I like the way you talk. The accent I mean. That Southern talk."

"It's very late."

She sat up attentively, without mockery, waiting.

"I can't" Giles said. "It's like when people put a microphone in your face or tell you to look natural for the camera. I can't do it. I have to go now."

"Wait. Please do wait." She was standing. Translucent panties. Short sheer gown. She talked comfortably as she dressed, gliding into jeans, pulling a loose shirt over the gown, buttoning it over her arms, then removing the gown from underneath.

"I'll drive," she said.

"No way."

"I love that, 'No way.' I like the way you say that, 'Noo Waay.' You can shift. Don't worry."

But he made her give him the keys, thinking he'd get money at his hotel, take her back to the apartment, then call a cab from there. He had time. He wouldn't be sleeping for a while. They drove a long time, the girl telling him when to turn here and there. They had left the oppressiveness of the apartment.

"I'm hungry," she said. "Pull in here."

"You've been taking me in circles, haven't you?"

"I've been watching you. I've been watching you going through the five-speed. I can do it now."

She ordered food for them. A waitress on roller-skates brought it to the car.

"They say you are what you eat."

"They're wrong," she said passing him a hamburger. "You become what eats you. Life in the food chain. I used to think we were food for angels."

"If your mother wakes, she'll wonder where you are. She'll be worried." The girl held up one finger as she chewed and swallowed.

"She never knows where I am. She worries all the time. She's a classic worrier. Someday they'll build a statue to her, call it The Great Mother of Worriers. I'll simply remind her of the Mississippi man. Now give me the keys."

He hesitated.

"Noo Waay," she said laughing. "How will I ever learn? How will I ever get back to Kansas, Toto?"

"Don't take your eyes off the road," he said. "Don't confuse changing gears with driving. Look away too long and you end in a ditch." Her hair blew across her face, but Giles could see that she was smiling.

"There isn't a ditch in this whole bloody city. I love you. You know that? I love you."

He held his hand on hers and performed the actual shifting until she had the feel of it.

"Only one last thing," she said. "I have to learn to command the radio, too."

"Save it," he said.

"Well, you command the radio, I'll do the driving."

The yellow haze of night was shifting to gray morning.

"What's the name of this one?" she said, nodding toward the radio.

"Everybody Wants To Rule The World."

"Who sings it?"

"Tears For Fears. It's old."

She turned and looked into his eyes, and he saw that she was just a little girl.

"And you remember it?" she asked.

"Yes," he said, turning his eyes from hers. "From college." He wanted to say something to her. She was waiting, but he couldn't find the words.

"Last stop, Lincoln's destiny," she said, steering the car to the curb outside the bar.

He didn't know what to say when they came to a stop. He didn't want to get out of the car, to just leave her there. For a second they both looked down at the radio, listening as the song began winding down, fading.

"Pretty good," he said, forcing a smile, "for an old song." The music floated from their open windows, out into the gray morning somewhere. Hers was the mask of a smile. He closed the door softly with both hands. He waited. She looked up at him. Then she looked away, out at the city.

"Nobody wants to rule the world," she said. "Nobody really wants to rule the world."

He looked at her eyes, at the blue and white and red lights of the city reflecting in them.

"I can go anywhere now, can't I?" she said glancing around the interior of the small car, avoiding his eyes, holding back. "Anywhere at all." She looked straight ahead, waiting for him to step away from the car.

For a time her eyes didn't move. Then she looked at him. "Can't I?" she said, gripping the steering wheel. "Anywhere."

She reached down to the radio and switched it off.

"Thanks," he said.

"For what?"

"You know, the ride."

"Think I can make it back home in one piece?"

"Absolutely."

"Say that again," she said, "that same way. That Southern way."

"Absolutely."

"Again," she said.

"Absolutely."

"You wanna bet?" she said.

Giles Carter tried hard to remember how long the walk had been from the hotel to the bar. He was walking in the right direction, but nothing looked familiar. He didn't know how far it was or how long it would take. Could be two blocks, two miles, two continents he thought. Then he knew it didn't matter. The earth could open up and swallow him at any moment. One day the earth *would* open up and swallow this city. It was only a matter of when.

Anything can happen, he thought. Anything can happen. Anything.

What You Really Mean Is
Rene Severance and Giles Carter

At some indecipherable moment in their conversation, she hung up on him. And after a dozen phone calls and as many messages on her machine, Giles Carter couldn't stand it. He drove from his Myrtle Beach hotel through the night to Florence seventy miles away, to Rene's apartment.

Passing the somber, Gothic hospital complex that marked the city limits, he lit another cigarette and lowered his window. The humidity washed over him like a heavy tide, and the salty air trapped in the car's interior was absorbed by the night, gone. The wipers peeled away the foggy film that materialized on the windshield. At red lights, he slowed, glanced both ways, then drove on. The dark voice of the tires' gripping the pavement whispered up from the damp streets. It was two-thirty in the morning.

He found her note tacked neatly at each corner, as perfectly centered as a painting on the new white door: *Call the police. Please don't be the one.*

He reached for the door. It was unlocked, and after easing it open he did take one step. Then called her name. He took another step, called again, and listened. Giles heard the sound of the bath upstairs.

This is how it began: Rene and Giles were first-year teaching assistants at Duke University. Coincidentally, they had each required their students to see *Carnal Knowledge*, the first campus film of the year. When they ran into one another in the lobby, it seemed only collegial to have coffee and talk. It was, they would say by Christmas, their first date.

The truest scene, they agreed, is when Jack Nicholson and Candice Bergen meet. In the scene, Nicholson and Bergen are driving to a small cafe and talking about how men and women communicate. Nicholson says that men and women speak in code, like spies. Everything means something else, he says. Bergen says, "Yes, and when you say that you mean something else." Nicholson says, "But when you say that what you really mean is..."

Rene and Giles agreed that the scene supported current critical theory that questioned the validity of language in the rendering of human relations. Words, they agreed, were inadequate, unreliable. He quoted Stanley Fish and she quoted Jacques Derrida and then they motioned for more coffee.

Rene, who had come to Duke to study Milton, assigned the film to her class titled "Failed Feminine Models and the New Woman." Giles, who had come because he admired Reynolds Price, said his students were reading from Robert Bly and would discuss Nicholson and Garfunkel as two incomplete sides of the male psyche.

"Just look at the women in the film," Rene said. "Count them. You have The Girl Next Door, Bergen. Big Boobs, Ann-Margret. The Cold Ball Buster, the Woman-Child hippie, and The Prostitute. All of them, they are all stereotypes. There are no other choices represented."

"Women in the audience are supposed to identify with Bergen," Giles said, pouring them more coffee, "because she has small breasts and gets to sleep with both guys, and yet remains a 'good girl'."

"That's Mr. Hollywood selling tickets," Rene said, reaching for her cup.

"But what you mean when you say that," Giles said, smiling, "is that the idea that a good girl would want to sleep with a man, two men, is a male, not a female fantasy."

"And what you mean when you say that—" Rene waited until he stopped smiling. "What you mean is you'd rather talk about sex than the movie."

"Meaning, really, that you are grateful I brought up the subject of sex, because you are a good girl who has fantasies of sleeping with two men as different as Nicholson and Garfunkel—has in fact slept with men very much like them—but you could never be the one to initiate the conversation. Because you are a good girl."

"Meaning, more to the point, that—by omission I might add—I have small breasts, but you wouldn't kick me out of bed." They both laughed.

"And what *you* mean when you say that is that it is time for me to say whether I would kick you out of bed before you reveal more of yourself in this conversation."

"But what you *really* mean is that you are not sure you can recapture the erection you had when Ann-Margret's tits filled the screen, and you'd rather I didn't sleep with you than experience failure again in bed."

"Which is another way of saying that if you threaten me with sexual failure, you won't have to experience the guilt of making love with me while fantasizing that I am alternately Nicholson and Garfunkel. When I'm on top it's Nicholson; when you're on top it's Garfunkel.

"Face it, Giles. You're a boob man."

They were both laughing now. "You're right. You got me." They were both laughing hard now. "And yet what you really mean when you say that is that"—he waited for her to catch her breath—"if you *did* have enormous boobs, you'd take a picture and send it to Jack Nicholson."

"God, yes," she said.

The next morning in the shower, they talked deconstruction. Before they were done, Rene had named his penis Derri and her breasts the Dadas.

At parties, when the conversation turned to gender issues, Rene and Giles derailed theoretical controversy, one spinning off the other's verbal gymnastics until the whole room was laughing. They quickly became famous among graduate students for their myths about a seventy-year-old one-armed albino woman blues singer who'd finagled a humanities grant to support her post-punk radical feminist trio, Derri and the Dadas. They were a hit. Someone suggested they begin renting themselves out for parties. That was in the winter of 1990.

Classes ended in May. For three weeks at the beach, they ate strawberries and sharp cheese, cold shrimp, sliced apples and boiled eggs. They drank Chablis that was eye-achingly cold. They took meals on their bed.

The sky was blue-black with heat and energy. The surf, the color of cracked slate, churned into whiteness at the shore. With the bitter smell of salt brine blowing over her in a misty fog, Rene gripped her hat with both hands against the sand and wind. Giles tossed chunks of bread that raced like meteors and brought the black-throated gulls so close to his head that she begged him to stop it. Huddled under the eaves a few feet away, she shouted through the hard wind and surf for him to stop it, running finally, pleading with him to kiss her.

During the late night, rain cascaded from the roof onto the porch outside their window, soothing them as they lay slick and breathless. Candlelight from the other room defined lips, illuminated nipples.

An evolving conversation interrupted only by sleep and lovemaking consumed their days. They bared adolescent dreams, described in hushed voices their deepest unexpressed fantasies, then later laid open their most savage secrets like conspirators, assassins, knowing-

-even anticipating the thrilling danger of their revelations, then purged their dark confessions always with wine and sex, followed by more talk. They turned each other inside out with talk.

Then in September, before the summer had quite folded upon itself, she stood in the black surf crying as he swam with all his strength toward the low, parched moon, hoping it would swallow him, pulling hard in the slanted current until it slammed him against the bits of shell that stretched like broken constellations at the frothy water's edge near the pier late in the night.

And neither of them could say how it had happened. They couldn't say how it had come to that.

They didn't speak for five years.

Giles applied all the charm and political energy he could muster and fake to selling his first novel. Still, when it was well received, he was so surprised by its moderate success that he couldn't mask feeling that he was an impostor. The book had been just good enough to make a brief splash, but when serious reviewers noted that Giles had studied under Reynolds Price they lamented that he'd not learned more from his teacher. At signings and other publisher-sponsored events, he sensed that every bookstore cashier, stock boy, and janitor was impatiently watching the clock and tapping his toe, waiting to switch off the lights, to pull up stakes before Giles could close his bag and button his jacket. When he couldn't write the second book, he gutted it, reformatted it and called it a screenplay. He made the rounds of writing conferences, vanity presses.

Waiting for a flight in the Atlanta airport on Christmas Eve, he'd looked up from his newspaper and glimpsed the spitting image of her thirty yards away. He raced to catch the woman, never thinking for a moment that she wouldn't be Rene.

Then in the spring, he received a birthday card, which finally caught up with him two weeks later and was delivered to his table tucked in the cleavage of a Hyatt cocktail waitress, whom he vaguely remembered sleeping with once.

The next month at a bookstore in Charlotte, he ran into an old Duke alumnus. Rene, the friend said, was teaching at a college in South Carolina and was married to a pharmaceutical salesman. Another year passed. He received a second card. There was no mention of her separation from her husband, Joshua, but a postscript noted that she could soon be reached at the return address, *her* new apartment. He ran his fingers over the carefully formed letters on the card, folded it and tucked it inside his jacket.

Giles called the police from his car phone, then waited, watching the digital minutes pass. He met the uniformed officer at the apartment door, but didn't go inside again. He pointed toward his car, said he'd wait there. Arriving without blue lights or sirens, three more cars parked out front. Officers smoked outside her apartment door and talked in low voices.

The neighbors slept.

At four o'clock, Giles watched as a policeman and a man in a dark suit and tie helped Joshua, Rene's husband, walk from the apartment, supporting him at his elbows. His hands covered his eyes. He bent forward like a very old man with his hands covering his face. His legs had buckled, as if he might fold up like an accordion. Giles wanted to drive away as soon as the officer took his name and told him he was free to leave. He sat alone, knowing that he had to hold to the covenant of not looking, that it was the only act of love left to him. He could not drive away. Giles looked down from his window, down at the new, bright yellow paint that cleanly marked each parking space on the wet, black asphalt, and he thought of the men who painted them, men who spent their lives painting clean, straight lines.

By the time he parked outside his Myrtle Beach hotel, the sky had become a bruised pink wash. The gulls glided low over the smooth, calm, gray water.

Inside, the doorman, a young man who wore an earring and kept his long red hair tucked under his cap, recognized him. "Morning, sir," he said, giving Giles a conspiratorial wink. "Vampire's life is hell, ain't it?" the young man said, grinning in collusion.

Giles Carter stepped into the elevator and reached absently for his room key, then turned to face the stainless steel doors closing silently before his eyes.

Giles sat through four bourbons at the Dallas airport that night long ago, thinking of phoning and not phoning. Then calling, only to get Rene's machine. Then hanging up when Joshua answered. Then after another bourbon, he called again.

She and Josh had just come in from dinner at a cafeteria, Rene told him. "There was this woman with her son," she said. "They were in front of us in the line. And the little boy put his arm around the woman and said, 'I love you, Mamma.' The woman pushed him away, saying, 'No, no, no.' And the boy put his hand up to the woman's face, and she rapped him hard on his head. I couldn't watch it."

Rene took a deep breath. "And then you could tell that the boy was retarded. He put his arms around his mother, holding her so tight that she couldn't step forward in line to get their food. She pushed him away, but he kept pawing at her, and you knew that he just never stopped, and the whole time he kept saying in his small voice, 'I love you. I love you.' And he *did*. And she had to live with that every day. He really did love her. You could see it. I'm not saying this right."

In the silence, Giles realized how many miles were between her voice and his.

"Just as she reached the trays, the boy said, 'I have to go to the bathroom, Mamma.' The woman had tears in her eyes. The two moved back past us. And you could tell this was her life. The boy put his arms around her, stopping her. He held her tight and smiled up at her. 'Happy Halloween, Mamma,' he said. 'Happy Halloween, Arnie,' his mother said."

For a time neither of them spoke. The silence traveled two thousand miles, turned, and traveled back. Then Rene was quietly sobbing. And he knew, holding the booth to steady himself, that he would never find the words to ask her, or to tell her. And it was in that way that it ended.

This Is Not A Love Story
George and Rita Scarborough

I'm not sure what shelf you might put this one on, but it's definitely not a love story. It turns out all wrong for a love story. Love stories leave you feeling that what you're missing inside still has a residence in there someplace—a tidy room with open windows and sunshine, crisp sheets on the bed, pictures of ripe fruit on the wall. Love stories make you hold your breath near the end. And if tears come to your eyes, you're thankful to have them. Don't expect any of that from this story. Expect disappointment.

You'll find no throbbing hearts or other parts here, no reconciliation. If you think you're going to witness a beautiful young woman who discovers a long-lost love letter from her once-betrothed who died in the war, forget it. Just in case you were hoping to read about some old codger whose estranged daughter returns after ten years with a crinkled black-and-white and a cheap cassette of the two of them singing "Jesus Loves Me" when the girl was three, prepare yourself to writhe and wretch when he's done with his lemonade. You've been warned.

Just so you'll know, I'm beginning with about the fourth or fifth tender moment in a conversation that started earlier in the day, a conversation that itself was about something else. This part opens with me and Rita in my pickup, traveling at 55 miles an hour, on our way to the church. It begins, as you might expect, with Rita, my one and only.

"If I could crank that chain saw, I'd cut you up and feed you to the hogs."

"And just where do you see a chain saw, Rita?" She was sitting like a statue, her back stiff, her eyes straight ahead, talking to the windshield.

"I know where you keep it, too," she said. "I know right where it is. It's out in the shop. It's hanging on a nail where I can reach it. The directions for cranking it are right there on the motor."

"If you took some reading lessons, I'd be in trouble, wouldn't I?"

"You're in trouble now, big boy, you're in deep doo-doo as we speak. If I was a little stronger, you'd be bacon next week."

With some people, anger brings on age. They look tired and worn. Not Rita. Her face was flush, her eyes clear and bright. Under different circumstances I'd have teased her, whispered where and when I'd seen that look before.

"Well, hell, Rita, why don't you just join that aerobics group at church, build up a muscle or two. Maybe the preacher'd take you off the line, make a running back out of you."

"You hateful thing," she said.

I told her I'd quit if she'd just take back what she'd said, the thing that wasn't true. She didn't speak.

"*You* started it this time," I said.   She wouldn't look at me. After a minute I began singing, "I love you, a bushel and a peck——."

"I hate your guts," she said.

Like I said, you might not call this a love story.

Sometimes I think the only thing Rita is capable of loving is softball. When she was young, she played third base. I've never seen a woman who could play the game—or fill out a uniform—like Rita. She's got twenty-year-old trophies out the wah-zoo. They line the top of the bookcase in our den. Softball's what brought us together.

We met the summer we were fifteen, when she'd come from town to help the Stricklands put in tobacco. She learned to drive the harvesting machine the first day on the job. Rita is not a woman without determination.

During those six weeks we fell into that dung pile called love. It all began on the same church league softball field we were driving to during the chain saw conversation.

In those days, I'd watch only her through the whole game, while she was on the field or on the bench, and especially at bat. She had a stance at the plate that I wish I had a picture of. Seven innings wasn't enough of her that summer.

Most nights after the last out of the seventh, I'd hurry across the bridge that connected Miss Brantley's yard and foul territory behind third base. Miss Brantley, who was old even then, donated a soybean field to the church for the diamond and paid the electric bill each month. When she came to the door, I'd ask her to please leave the lights on and offer her five dollars of my tobacco money. By the end of that summer, she'd be standing at the door when I came up on her porch. She'd smile, nod, and refuse to take my money.

I'd hit Rita grounders for an hour or more—one-hoppers down the line, soft miss-cues like bunts, line drives, choppers, hard shots to her left and right. She was errorless, that young, lean girl.

When we'd both had enough, we sat on the bench and she made shapes in the sand with her spikes as we talked. Maybe an hour or more, just the two us, alone. I knew, sitting there beside her, that by the end of the summer she'd be as tanned as a butternut squash. I came to know the smell of her sweat.

There's something about sitting on the bench of a softball field, with the lights on, late at night when there are no sounds, feeling a cool summer breeze, watching bugs hurling themselves like lunatics around the lights in the outfield. The light is brighter than day, the dark darker than night. There are clean lines around everything. Everything's in your eyes. Nothing really makes sense, or needs to. It was on one of these late nights that summer when we were fifteen that Rita gave me her ring.

And it was on that same field I lost it. I mean, really lost it. I mean *looked every square inch of the infield for it, covered that same ground with a yard rake* lost it. Then after three afternoons alone combing the field, I reached down for no known reason, sifted my fingers through the warm, loose sand and found it, there in front of the bench where we'd sat those nights. I slid it back onto my little finger.

Two weeks later, at the end of tobacco season, after the barbecue dinner and the last of the little brown envelopes that held our pay, when she was about to go back to town for the last time, I told her about losing the ring and finding it. She said it was destiny. And she never gave up until I said I'd marry her.

Now—as you can see—there's maybe more lemon than sugar in our tea. But the power of habit, even between people who can't stand the sight of each other, is a powerful thing. So I drive Rita to all the games. They are her only happiness.

From June to August, that's where you'll find us. Saturday nights, there are at least two games. The women play first. Rita sits with her knees up to her chin and the tips of her fingers pressed into her mouth. She watches every pitch, knows the possible consequences of every play. She doesn't talk or even look at me. But when the score is close in the late innings, she'll sometimes reach for my hand and squeeze it. And once in a while when I've left and returned unnoticed from the concession stand with a cold drink, I'll touch her leg. She'll look over at me, see the drink I'm offering, and smile with eyes so bright you'd never understand.

But now we were driving to the field. I turned on my blinker, as required by law, steered into the church lot, and parked across from old Miss Brantley's shed.

"And just why, pray tell, are you parking way back here?" Rita said.

"Cause when the game's over I want to get home lickety-split, *comprendez?*"

She just huffed, surveyed the distance to the playing field and back, then looked over at me, like I was supposed to mind-read her calculations.

"You're just being mean."

I waited for her to open the door, then hit the starter. She pulled the door to, looking ahead like the Queen of the Hill. I parked right behind the backstop, where a foul ball might find our windshield. And she knew it. She glared over at me with schoolteacher scorn.

"We'll be the last ones out," I said like a crooner, giving her cow eyes. "Just think, you and me, alone, here in the truck. It could take hours."

She slammed the door behind her.

"Take it back, Rita," I shouted as she was walking away. "All you got to do it take it back. You don't have to say you're sorry." She didn't even break stride. "Sometimes winning ain't winning," I said to the backside of her. "Just say you didn't mean it."

By the bottom of the second with two outs, she was her old self again, following every pitch, plotting every move. She leaned my way, not taking her eyes from the game, nodded toward the batter who was digging in, and whispered, "If she's got sense enough to hit it to the opposite field, she'll score the runner on second." When the batter took first base on four straight balls, she pulled her knees in tight against her chest. "It's situations like this," she said, trailing off. "It's times like these, in the early innings sometimes—" she whispered. "They don't even know it, but tomorrow or next week they'll look back and see that it was won or lost right here, right now."

With the bases loaded and three balls and no strikes, the batter swung at a pitch outside the strike zone and hit a soft liner to third. It was all over. Rita brought her hands up to her face, took a deep breath, and went back to the game.

In the top of the fourth a wave of cool air hushed the crowd, and between innings raindrops the size of quarters dotted the infield.

"Let's go to the truck," I said, lifting my cushion. Rita put hers over her head.

"I'll give it a minute," she said.

Before I could shut the truck door behind me, the world was gray. I reached over to the other door and pushed it open when I saw the outline of Rita running toward me. We watched the rain as it came down on the infield, making blooming spikes of the water that already covered the playing area. I watched as Rita slowly turned and tilted her head, sopping her hair with a thin, red scarf from her big straw handbag, her brown, high cheekbones beaded with rain, her full lips wet. The cold rain wet the skin through her thin blouse. If I had known what to say, I would have said it.

When the storm let up a little, the engines started and we watched as drivers cleared the inside of their windshield with their sleeve, their wipers going flippity-flop like a fast-motion movie. Everybody looked like teenagers, their wet hair down, their suntanned faces shiny, their eyes alert and excited because something unexpected had made them scramble and laugh at one another in their clumsy attempts to beat the summer rain.

The jaggedly parked cars began to slowly turn, turn again, and then creep like a slow train toward the highway. The bright field looked like a smoke cloud.

I slid the key into the ignition.

"And just what are you doing?" Rita said, looking at me for the first time.

"W-E-L-L," I said. "Let's make this a game. You get three guesses."

She reached over and shut off the engine, pulled out the key.

"It might stop in a minute."

"Did you bring your ball and glove, Rita? Cause just in case you haven't noticed, there ain't going to be anybody but you and me to play when the tide goes out, sweet pea."

Rita's eyes scoured the field, studying it, considering all the possibilities. The last car pulled out of the church drive.

And then the rain stopped. As suddenly and unexpectedly as the shower had come, it was gone. We sat there without a word. In a matter of seconds it was over, no random drops, no lingering mist, gone.

I looked at her again, the rain on her face, her eyes the color of blue metal against her deep tan. The thin, soaked blouse.

"What you said, it's not true, Rita."

She looked over at me as if I'd woke her from sleep, slapped her the instant she opened her eyes.

"Oh, shut up," she said. "Shut up."

"It's a lie."

She reached for the door.

"You're so stubborn, all you really care about is being right— even when you know you're wrong." She was about to speak, but I cut her off. "Why did you say what you did?" She answered my question by hurling the door shut. She was crossing home plate by the time I got out of the truck, and headed for center field by the time I was within calling distance. Thunder vibrated the ground.

"If you think I never loved you, you are wrong, you hard-head." She was still walking, near the outfield grass now. "Besides, what makes you think you're so high and mighty that you could *ever* make me do anything I didn't want to do. Give me one example of that over the past twenty years, just one." She shouted something I couldn't make out over the rumble, yelling toward deep-center, picking up her pace a little. I was at the mound. "I'd never have married you if I didn't love you." She didn't look back. "It's been twenty years, Rita." She said something that I just know was cussing, but I couldn't tell which combination of words. "Well aren't we full of *ourselves*!" I yelled back. I'd made it to the edge of the outfield grass. "So where do you think you're going, Miss Power Queen!"

Now she stopped, turned and waited for me to make up a few steps.

"I'm going home," she said in a nearly normal voice. Her hair was down to her eyes, and her blouse stuck like cellophane. Rita summoned all her strength.

"Well, *I'm* sure as hell not walking," I shouted. "You can walk by yourself."

"Fine," she said, turning. She took maybe three steps, then stopped cold. She looked down into her hand, then up at me. "Here," she yelled, suddenly throwing my keys as hard as she could. I saw the keys arch, then fall between us. Rita turned and marched toward the center field fence.

"This ought to be good," I yelled, trailing again. "I can't wait to see this," I shouted. "This is gonna be priceless." I looked over at the spot where the keys had landed. "Let's see Miss-know-it-all-I-am-never-wrong clear the wall like the queen of women's prison. Better get a good running start there, sugar pie."

I stopped and watched as she neared the fence.

"I can do things you never even dreamed I could do."

She reached for the top of the fence with both hands, pulled, and pushed up hard with both legs. She threw one elbow over the lip of the fence, pulled and nearly hooked the other elbow, banging the wall, then caught the top again with her free hand. Her feet dangled, thumped the wooden fence. She hung still and silent for a second. This wasn't funny. Then with a grunt she threw up her right leg, clearing the fence with her heel. She again pressed hard with her left elbow, hung there horizontally suspended, then came down on her back with a jarring splash.

I ran as hard as I could through the thick, soggy grass. She wasn't moving. I fell to my knees beside her. She was crying like a little girl. I reached down for her. But she pushed my hand away and tried to kick me in the shin when I stood.

At second base, I put my hand around her waist, and she put one hand on my shoulder. She was crying again, giving it up in little lurches. And I was crying too, but I turned away so she wouldn't see.

By the time we got to the mound, a thick mist covered everything.

We were both soaked. I took her hand at home plate. She waited as I opened the truck door for her and didn't say a word as she slid onto the seat.

The cab windows were already foggy from the heat of Rita's body by the time I shut the door behind me. The rain had begun again.

I dug for my keys.

We sat without a word; then I reached for my wallet. It was sopping wet.

"Here," Rita said, offering me a dry five dollars from her straw bag.

When old Miss Brantley came to the screen door, I'm sure she didn't recognize me. I held up the five and asked if she'd mind leaving the lights on for a while. She smiled, then slowly nodded as if there was something pleasing going on in her head. She turned and waddled back down the long hall.

The rain was really coming down now, and I had to rely on memory to make my way through the darkness that was Miss Brantley's backyard, past the canopy grapevine to the narrow bridge, over the wide, deep, rushing ditch, on over to the lighted diamond. I tilted my head against the rain and followed my own steps back toward the field. I'd crossed the third base foul line before I looked up to see Rita, sitting on the bench alone, in the bright, bright light with the rain pouring down, waiting for me. She turned and I saw her wet face, her eyes in that light. Twenty years disappeared.

We'd have another hour or more to search for the keys, I thought. There was a chance that we'd find them, both of us really looking with all we had, taking our time. We might find them.

But the odds were against it.

Sunspots
Robyn Couch

I'm supposed to get off at three a.m., but the other girl who works the drive-thru hardly ever gets here on time. I've quit asking her why. The fact is I can use the overtime, and it's hard for me to sleep anyway. The exit I take is only about twelve miles down, so I don't really mind the extra wait. It's always a quiet drive, especially after listening to the squawking of those little speakers for nine or ten hours, and I like it. I don't even turn on the radio, usually. And of course it's real dark, and there's nothing to take my eyes away from my headlights. Except on those nights when there's a breakdown. Strange thing is, some nights you'll see three, maybe even four vehicles pulled over. Sometimes they have their blinkers on—which is kind of spooky—sometimes not. I look for people who may be stranded, but there's never anybody there. I can't figure out why, on just certain nights, there would be so many breakdowns. It's not something you can blame on the weather.

My daddy says it's sunspots. He quit selling CBs a couple of years ago because he said there was going to be a fit of sunspots that would ruin everybody's reception. Sunspots, he says. I think it's something else.

Hardly anybody likes working the drive-thru, especially the graveyard shift. You have to listen with concentration, and sometimes you have to figure out what people want. Sometimes they don't speak toward the speaker, sometimes they don't talk like people from around here, sometimes they just don't know what they want. It's important to get it right. The drive-thrus get madder than the walk-ins if you make a mistake. The owner—Cale Yarborough, the race car driver—says the front office don't care all that much that people love the food. It's making them mad you don't want to do. So some people don't last long at the drive-thru. I've been on it for two years though.

My trick is to learn everything on the menu. Not just what it is, but how it sounds. Then you try to think of all the possible ways to say a thing. It keeps your mind alert to try to hear all the possible ways people end up saying things. That's my secret anyway.

I like it too because I don't have to look busy when I'm not. I don't have to wipe down the counters, or change the oil for the fries, or mop the floors till the end of my shift. My window faces out at I-95, and sometimes I sit for long stretches and watch the headlights of people on their way somewhere. Sometimes I daydream.

Another reason why the other girls don't like working the drive-thru is because of the customers we get real late–tired old folks from New York or Florida or spoiled teenagers, or drunks who talk in Donald Duck voices. They don't get to me though. Sometimes I meet some pretty interesting people, really. You would be surprised how much you can tell about a person in the time it takes them to dig up correct change. You can look down in their car and tell all sorts of things about them. Whether they like things neat and clean, what kind of music they like by their tapes, what they smoke if they smoke. Where they have been or where they are going.

All of life passes by the drive-thru. I've had newly-weds with shaving cream all over their car order Cherry Cokes, and couples on their way home with a new baby order milkshakes. Once a hearse came to the window, fully loaded, and another time I saw a pistol under a grocery bag on the seat of a Cadillac with New Jersey tags. People who have been crying always order coffee.

Some days I'll decide I'm going to look every customer square in the eye. It's like a project. Some don't like it and look away. But others smile or say hello. I don't stare, you know. I just say to myself, you got eyes, look at somebody's eyes. And it is like that message travels down to people in their cars. There's something about looking at people. There's something to it.

Sometimes, more often than you'd think, you can tell if they are happy people or not. You'd be surprised how easy it is. You can tell how a man and woman look at each other. Or don't. How they talk to their kids, if they do. Most times it's like being invisible when you stand at that window and look down into people's cars. You can tell a lot about them, you really can. Some you like instantly. You don't know why, but you do. A young man will sit there unfolding money–he might be going north or going south–and I know I'd like him and I say, "Traveling?" And he'll smile and tell me where he's going to or coming from. Usually, that's all there is to it. But other times I'll still be thinking about him when he leaves the access ramp and joins the traffic. Sometimes longer.

I took the job after Houston left. He sent money for a while. But not long. And Momma finally agreed to keep April for me so long as it was when she was sleeping. So this is really perfect. I've got my high school diploma. I could probably do better, but for now I'm doing okay.

Houston used to say there were things he wished he could say to me but he just couldn't. That didn't make sense to me. I don't know why it should be so hard. Either you love somebody or you don't. And if you love somebody you just open your mouth and say so, and if you don't you got the same mouth to say it with. He never said he didn't love me. He just left. Some say it was having April. I think it was something else.

People up North are surprised that it gets really cold this far south. But it does. I don't look forward to working then. I never seem to get warm at the window. When I first started, I'd go out a few minutes before getting off work and warm up the car. But it really is a waste of gas money. I only live twelve miles away. But those are some cold nights, when you are cold all the way through and your teeth clack. I still think the heater will someday warm up, but for now the blower just blows cold air.

It's the bridges that ice over first. Funny, it's warm here most of the time, but those signs, Bridge Ices Before Road, are always up as reminders. True, we don't get much snow. What we get is ice. Ice is worse. Ice is more dangerous. It's ice that does the damage. What you have to look out for.

It's on these nights that I ought to stop when I see a car pulled over. Somebody could freeze to death. It's happened before. But I don't. It's not that I'm really afraid. Sure it's spooky. But I'm not really scared of much. I wish I'd stop. But I don't. I can't say why.

I try to decide what I'm going to think about on the drive home before I clock out, button up my car coat, pump the accelerator twice and hit the starter. It helps to have that in my head before I go to the car. Then when the cold gets to my bones, I steer my mind back to that thought. I used to think about Houston and me a lot the first winter I worked here, and about how things were when we very first got married. But I hardly ever think about him now. Really. But sometimes I do think that if I met a guy and if I came to fall in love with him, I would sure say so. It just don't seem that complicated to me. Maybe it's where I come from. But to me, saying I love you just isn't that hard to say. I think it makes me a happier person.

Flat-Out
Evander Baker, Robyn Couch, and Marion Walker

I walked out of church after Wednesday night prayer meeting and saw that somebody had slashed the tires on my Corvette. I'd parked it off a ways under the bare branches of a ragged water oak, out near the road, safely away from the other cars. When the prayer service was done, I stepped out on the landing to have a cigarette. That's when I saw the 'vette all hunkered down on the ground, moon shadows falling across the car like a hungry spider clutching and sucking the life from it. I wanted to kill somebody.

The next day, I called my sister Maurine and told her about the tires. Her TV was up, and I could tell by her end of the conversation that she wasn't paying me any mind. At one point, I just listened to her TV. Neither of us spoke for what must have been five minutes. Then she started crying and I hung up.

After I reported the crime to my boss at HAPPY VIDEO, I went outside and sat on the trailer steps with a glass of tea. There wasn't a cloud in the sky. It would have been a good day for riding around. I slid my fat ass over to the corner of the steps out of the wind and leaned back into the light and fell asleep.

Everything was gray when I woke. My face was cold and the step I'd been laying against had left a deep cleft in the small of my back. I grabbed the rail to raise myself up. Before I could get to my feet, my sister pulled into the drive. She brought chocolate chip cookies, and we buried them in the back yard.

Maurine put me in a bad mood right off by insisting I dig the hole as near the septic line as possible. The ground was damp and warm from the sewer water, and I dug in big chunks. When I lifted the shovel, it made sucking sounds and sent the smell straight up my nose. Then to make things worse, Maurine tossed her cigarette butt in the hole, which sort of pissed me off. It just didn't seem right. I dished the cigarette filter from the bottom of the hole and gave Maurine a wicked look.

"Goddammit, Evander, I'm making a statement here," she said.

From habit I looked for fishing worms, but this was February.

When I was done, Maurine laid her head way back slowly and spoke to the gray sky with her eyes shut. "Valentines Day," she said, dragging out each letter, their sounds rising and falling exactly as if she were saying, Oh Mighty One. "Valentines Day," she said again in that sweating and crying voice.

The hole was almost two feet deep, more than enough grave for a bag of cookies, so I speared the shovel into the ground. She was still communicating with the spirits, head back, eyes closed, the cookies clutched against her tits. It was getting to be just a little bit too much show. "Hand 'em here," I said, reaching for the bag. She looked down at the chocolate chip cookies like they were a puppy or something and kind of shied away from me.

"Suit yourself," I said. I turned and slapped the handle of the shovel, sending it to the ground, and started back toward the trailer. "Evander!" she cried out. She was holding the cookies at arm's length. I snatched the bag, slam-dunked it into the hole, and in three scoops had the stinky dirt back where it belonged. Maurine stood with her back to me.

"There," I said, dragging the shovel behind me as I passed her. She was looking down at her feet like somebody had just pissed on her shoes, her lip all poked out.

It was a sad sight.

"Come on, honey," I said softly to Maurine. "Let's have a liquor drink." She squeezed up her cheeks and big tears bubbled out. "I never even opened the bag," she said, choking out every word. I put my arm around her shoulder and we started inside.

Maurine sat at the kitchen table mopping her eyes with a wad of toilet paper as I poured. "Look," I said, "why don't I come over to your trailer before it gets dark and help you get the Christmas lights down from the satellite dish?"

"Thank you, honey," she said, taking the drink from me. "I just don't think I'm ready yet, though. Steve and me, we put those up together."

"We just buried his cookies, for Christ's sake," I said.

"I know, I know," she said after taking a long drink. "But I'm just not ready yet." She handed me her glass for a refill, and I carried it over to the refrigerator and took out another ice tray.

Full coverage–that's comprehensive and collision–$900 every six months, $1800 a year. Tack on a $250 deductible for each claim.

Make a claim and watch your rates go up. And what you don't get is towing. Towing is extra. I called, asked to speak with the head guy at the office. He told me the same thing as my agent. You have to pay extra for towing. So the black 'vette sits in the church yard, flat on its belly all day Thursday while I talk to insurance criminals and the sheriff's office on the phone.

"Probably some kids," says the deputy, like I ought to just expect a dose of vandalism in my ordinary day. When I ask what he's going to do about it, he says, "We can't be everywhere at once, you know," like I'm supposed to just nod and sigh and pat the son-of-a-bitch on the back and feel sorry for the overworked old turd. Then he says he'll have to fill out a report, wants to know when I can *meet* him at the church. Those shitheads.

When I reminded him that I had no wheels, he said he didn't like my tone of voice.

"You're an Earnhardt fan, aren't you?" he said.

"You damned right I am," I said. He was getting personal now, which really pissed me off.

"Well, I suggest you get that hunk-O-junk outta there," he said, "before somebody steals your rims." He was laughing when I hung up.

The deputy's voice kept running through my head, and by Thursday night, I was wanting to wring somebody's neck. About that time, the preacher, who talks a good sermon but is a squirrelly loser, calls to tell me that the 'vette is a blemish on the church grounds and wants to know what I'm going to do about it. Just the way he says it sets me on fire. I'm about one second from unloading on that piss-ant when I see headlights coming up the drive.

Maurine rolls down her window and sticks her head way out and yells over the music. "Lock the door," she says, "and ride to town with me." She's wearing a red sweater she's had since junior high and so much perfume my eyes water. Still, I can smell the dope in her hair. But I don't say anything. She slows down as we coast past the church and our eyes follow the sleeping 'vette as we go by.

"I have something for you," Maurine says, "in a bag in the back seat." She gives me a stoned but sweet smile. "For helping me bury my past yesterday," she says. I'm thinking it's probably a bag of cookies, so I don't make the effort.

Maurine smiles again and begins to sing to the radio. At the first stoplight she looks in the mirror and watches her lips move to the lyrics. She pulls into a space in front of The Paradise Lounge, where we all drink, and shuts off the engine. Steve, her X, has parked his pickup a few spaces over. I reach for the door handle. "Uuh, uuh," she says, digging in her purse with one hand and motioning toward the back seat with the other. She's putting on a double dose of lipstick when I open the bag. "They're for you," she says. "For the dash of your car, for when you get it fixed."

There are twelve heads in the bag, her whole collection of Baby Alive baby doll heads.

"I wanted to find a way to say I was sorry about your car. I was only thinking about me yesterday. I know how much your car means to you, Evander." Maurine felt around in the bag. "Look at that happy smile," she said, holding up one of the heads. "You can glue them someplace and you'll never be alone or unhappy in your car. Now come inside and dance with me."

I take a seat beside Timmy Couch, the produce guy, at the bar. His sister, Robyn Couch, went with me to the junior-senior seven or eight years ago. She was the first girl I felt up. I've always been a little on the heavy side.

Timmy and I watched Clemson basketball on the TV behind the bar, and laughed at George Miles, the bartender, who pushed his eyelids up into his sockets so that his eyeballs bulged like a fish. I heard Maurine's voice behind me.

"Hey, George, I'll show you my titty if you'll bring my brother here a pitcher of beer before sometime next week." I could tell from her tone that she was one mad woman. George sprang to full attention and saluted grandly, his stiff fingers pressed beside his lidless bug eyes.

One night at this very bar a little cheerleader type had spilled beer on Maurine twice and then asked my sister what she planned to do about it. Everybody expected Maurine to baptize the girl. But instead, she tilted the girl's glass so that the beer ran out like wax on a floor, and in half a second she'd snatched the girl by the back of her head and slammed her face into the bar, bam bam.

"What's wrong?" I said to Maurine. Her eyes were darting all around the bar and her hands and feet were treading water. George put the pitcher and a mug in front of me. She pushed the pitcher in toward me, slid the mug back toward George.

"Drink," she said. I looked at her and lifted the pitcher. Before I got to the bottom, my sister ordered a six-pack to go.

"We're leaving," she said. Maurine and I had had our share of falling outs, and I wasn't about to start one now.

Before I could get my seatbelt on, Maurine jammed the car into reverse and squalled out of the parking space. She shifted the gears, and I felt that good feeling of being pressed back into the soft seat. Without taking her eyes from the road, she tore off three of the beers from the six-pack, popped the tops, and handed two of them to me. It felt good to be racing out of town.

"That two-timing dickhead," she said. Then she looked over at me. "Drink," she said.

I'd almost finished the second beer when we coasted into Steve's driveway. The house was dark and empty. "Finish up," she said, nodding toward the beer in my hand. I tilted it up and Maurine opened her door. As soon as I stepped out of her car, I turned my back to pee. "Don't you do it," Maurine threatened. She was holding up the key to Steve's house and making for the door. "Come on," she said.

I hadn't realized until I started toward Maurine how drunk I was. By the time I got up the steps, she already had the door open. She took my hand and led me through the dark living room, through the kitchen, to a little laundry room where the moonlight came through the window. She dropped my hand and opened the dryer door.

"There," she said, pointing into the dryer then turning her back. I stepped a little closer and unzipped my pants, feeling like I was standing on a boat. When I was done, Maurine turned the dial to More Dry, shut the door and pressed the start button.

It's funny what pulls people together, keeps them together. For twelve years Marion Walker hated me. He played tricks on me at school and called me names on the school bus. After graduation, he went to work at his old man's wrecker service. I didn't miss him calling me a fat ass or farting on the bus and then pointing at me. But as it turns out, him and Maurine and me are the biggest Dale Earnhardt fans in this town. Marion and me weren't really friends, but when I told him on the phone about the four slashed tires on the black 'vette, it was like we had a common enemy. I described to him my calls to the insurance crooks and the deputy, and he punctuated the conversation with, "those bastards," and "that low-down dog." Marion even offered to come by my trailer and pick me up. But I told him Maurine could take me to the church if he'd meet us there. She owed me.

"I'm takin' em down," Maurine said on the phone.

"What'd you say?" There was a lot of static on her portable phone.

"I'm out here taking down the Christmas lights," she said, "off the dish."

When Maurine and I pulled into the church drive, she laid her head to the side and brought the car to a quick stop. "Something ain't right," she said.

"No shit," I said, looking at the black, lame 'vette.

"No. Not the tires. Something else," she says in that the-spirits-are-speaking-to-me-voice.

We just sit there a second when we see Marion's wrecker coming up the road. Maurine pulls up near the 'vette and Marion pulls alongside, and I'm four feet from the driver's side with my key in my hand before I realize somebody's busted out my window. I can't believe it. I really can't. "Somebody busted out my goddamn window," I say. I can't believe it. I'm walking around like those guys in Vietnam movies who've just had their arm blown off and stagger around staring at their nub.

Marion steps over and looks inside. "Evander," he says, then looks down. I look over at Maurine and I know she wants to kill, too. "Bad news, Evander," Marion says, stepping away from the broken window. I look inside the car and see that the cassette player has been ripped from the dash.

I feel the veins throbbing in my temples. Maurine takes hold of my arm with both hands, leans her cheek toward my shoulder, and rocks softly. "Shhhhhh," she says, "Shhhhhhhh."

"Ain't nothing to do but get what's left of this baby on wheels and get the hell out of here," says Marion. He starts over toward the wrecker, head down like a bull fighter who's done his deed.

"Goddammit, somebody's gonna pay," I say in a voice that doesn't sound like mine.

"Don't use that language, Evander," Maurine said, dropping hold of my arm, "not at the Lord's house."

'I look at the thousands of glass pebbles in the front seat. "I'm gonna kill somebody," I say.

Marion returns with a wooden block incline, drops to his knees and places the sharp end up against, what used to be the left front tire. "We got to get it up a few inches to get the jack in. Start it up and give it just enough gas to roll it up on the block." Marion slides down on his side and gives the block a sharp kick.

I open the passenger door, look back at Maurine, then rake the glass out of the seat.

"The preacher is gonna love that," Maurine says, looking at all the glass on the ground.

"Fuck him," I say.

"Shame on you."

I put the key in the ignition, and Marion and my sister take a step back, like they're half expecting the thing to blow. Only guess what? Nothing happens. I turn the key and nothing happens.

"Go ahead," Marion says, "fire it up."

"What the hell you think I'm trying to do, spank my damned old dead monkey?" I'm about at my limit now.

"Pull the hood latch," Marion says, reaching for a rag in his back pocket. He lifts the hood and I hit the ignition again. "Forget it," Marion says, bringing the hood back down. "They stole your battery."

Now I'm pacing like a rabid dog, smoking like a fiend. Marion is wiping his hands in his rag, and Maurine has her chin in her palm, studying the car.

"Gotta have a battery," Marion says finally. "Can't do a thing without a battery." And then Maurine goes into this low wail and starts to rock on her heels like a retard. "Ooooooh. . . .Ooooooh," she says. Her eyes are all blank and staring into the face of the 'vette, and Marion and I exchange looks and then turn back to Maurine, who's gone mental on me. We look from the 'vette to Maurine, then back to the 'vette. Then I see. The license plate, the black number three license plate on the front of my car, the air-brushed Dale Earnhardt license plate–is gone.

Marion has a fifth of Jim Beam and a full tank of gas, so we ride to Darlington, park the wrecker across from Harold Brasington's famous track, and drink and smoke cigarettes for a while. We stare out at the track and trade Earnhardt stories. For a while I forget about the 'vette. Then Marion mentions the wife and kids, and we're rolling again. He offers to take me back to my trailer, but it's way past suppertime already. I tell him he can just drop me off at The Paradise Lounge, which is right on the way.

"Saturday night," Marion says, pulling to a stop. "You just might get lucky, Evander." He's looking into the bar's window. "Me, it's Saturday night with the wife and kids."

"Come on inside," I say. "Let me buy you just one drink."

"Nah," he says. "It's not so bad."

When I walk in the door at The Paradise Lounge, every eye in the place turns on me like scorecards at the Olympics. Word is out about my car. And as I wait for George Miles to draw my first beer, I'm just sure as hell people are whispering and laughing. I'm not in the mood for anything funny, not one bit.

George sets a beer in front of me. "I think you bought the last round, Evander," he says. "This one's on me, Bo." Then he bends over the bar. "Don't look now," he says man-to-man, "but we got a whole new world of possibilities here." He nods over toward the jukebox, and I see Robyn Couch, whose tits, like the rest of her, are bigger than I remember. "Free at last, free at last," George says, which is his way of saying she is divorced. Robyn is sitting alone.

George can tell, I guess by the look on my face, that I'm not feeling too confident, and he begins a story about when he got drunk at Myrtle Beach and picked up a midget at a night club. He wiggles his fingers as a way of describing the midget's legs jutting out from the front seat of his car. Then someone beside me speaks.

"Hey, Evander. You don't remember me, do you?" I'm as surprised as I am drunk, and I can't speak. "You took me to the prom, remember?"

Robyn's face is close to mine, and she is so clean and neat. She smells brand new.

For I don't know how long the 'vette disappears from my mind. It's just me and Robyn, and I open my mouth and the words come out and she laughs and takes my hand and says, "Oh, Lord, Evander, I'd forgot."

Beers arrive. Everybody at The Paradise Lounge seems so happy and my favorite Eagles' songs play on the jukebox. At some point, Robyn lays the warm palm of her hand against the side of my face and looks at me with shiny, shiny eyes and says, "Oh, yes," and everything goes away.

Sometime later, Robyn says she's going to the bathroom. George has his eyelids rolled back into fish eyes and he's doing the boogaloo behind the bar and people are laughing and singing.

Then I spot Steve, Maurine's ex-fiancé, come in the door. I look at him in his Jeff Gordon T-shirt and think about how much my sister loved him and about her crying on the phone after he sent her the chocolate chip cookies for a Valentine's present. My heart begins to do a one-eighty. He catches my eye and heads straight for me.

Maybe it's my imagination, but he smells like ammonia.

"Is Maurine here?" he says.

"No. And if she was–"

"We got something to straighten out. I really got to see her, Evander."

I'm thinking he's looking for a way to get even for his dryer.

"What you really got to do is leave her the hell alone."

"I have something for her. I gotta find her." His eyes are scouring the bar. I see Robyn heading my way from across the room.

"What'd you have for her this time, dog biscuits?"

"Fuck you, and your dog," he says, looking, I think, at Robyn.

Then everything goes white.

One of the rescue squad guys is standing over Steve, who's still lying on his back near the poker machine. Robyn's hands cover her mouth and her mascara looks like Alice Cooper's. The music has stopped and the whole crowd is watching the deputy put the cuffs on me. My cheek feels like an apple is growing out of it.

As I'm led toward the door, somebody shouts, "I found it!" and hands over a small box to Steve, who is sitting up by this time. He opens the box as the deputy leads me to the door. Then he looks up at me with sad, sad eyes, and I see the little diamond resting in his hand.

The deputy doesn't say anything on the way to jail, but he slows down to about five miles an hour as we drive past the church. Slow enough that I can see the figure of a man sitting behind the wheel of the 'vette.

When I wake up, I'm rolling again. I can see the outline of the morning at the edge of the dead fields. At first I think I must be in Robyn's car. It smells like a woman. But then I see that it's Marion Walker who has bailed me out of jail. He's driving his wife's Honda, which I've never seen him in before. I remember thinking that's funny, and I think I even smiled, then I was asleep again.

.

First thing Sunday morning, my boss from HAPPY VIDEO calls. I'm still a little drunk when I answer, and all I remember is I'm fired when I hang up the phone. I'm asleep again when the phone rings a second time, only this time it's the preacher calling me from church saying he hates to inform me but somebody has broken out my window and stolen my cassette player.

"Battery, too." I say.

"Beg your pardon?" the preacher says.

"And the Earnhardt plate."

There is a long pause. Then he asks if I want to pray for my car, and I say yes and he does the honors for two or three minutes. There is another long pause. He asks if I feel better, and I say I do. Then he starts something that sounds like I Told You So and I hang up.

The next time I wake up, somebody's in my room. I pull the pillow from my face and see Maurine with her back to me, going through my closet.

"Oh, hey, Evander," she says, holding up my black suit which still has the plastic from the cleaners. "Get up now. I've got a surprise for you."

When I walk out from showering and shaving, Maurine has come back from the store with a Pepsi and a honeybun for me.

She makes sure my tie is on straight, and we head for her car. In the back seat, folded in half, is a near life-size cut-out of Dale Earnhardt. "I got it from the Sav-Way yesterday," she says. "I put it in your car last night, behind the wheel, just in case anybody driving by got any funny ideas."

The old guy at Olan Mills is very professional about everything. Maurine gives him the discount coupon, tells him what she wants, and sends me to the car for the Earnhardt cut-out. The guy is positioning the stools for us to sit on when I come back in. He takes Dale from me and props him just so using an extra tripod behind the stools, then sits Maurine and me down, squares up our shoulders, and turns my face so the bruise won't show. Earnhardt is smiling over us.

After the guy has snapped the first couple of pictures, he tells us to relax and take a deep breath. Maurine looks over at me and smiles.

"This was a nice surprise, wasn't it, Evander?" She leans over and hugs me a little bit, and the photographer catches the moment.

I look back at Dale. Then I think about the license plate and the 'vette, then Marion Walker and George Miles, and Maurine. I think about Steve. And finally about Robyn Couch and the way her hand felt on my face.

My heart starts swelling up, and I feel like I'm someplace else when Maurine gives me a little tug.

"Smile, Evander, honey," she says. "You look like you're about to cry."

Wrecker
Marion Walker

The truth is complicated. I don't mean knowing it. Knowing it isn't so hard, sometimes. But getting it told can be next to impossible. The more you try to say it, the farther from it you get. Like pushing the same ends of a magnet towards one another, the more words people say to one another the farther they get from what they are trying to say, until you hear stuff coming out of your mouth and you say to yourself, where the hell did that come from? Or the other person says, what do you mean? And the fact is, you don't have the slightest idea what you mean. Then you get into the explaining, and before it's over the two of you are pushing each other across Colorado when you both know the truth lives in Carolina. Sometimes it's just better to keep your mouth shut.

It's not that you don't know the truth. It's just that when you do know something, and you know that it's true and somebody tells you to explain or to give examples, it just ruins it. We all know some things that are true. It's the telling that gets in the way. But when you love somebody, and you know it's true, and still she wants you to explain to her what love is, the telling screws up the thing you're trying to say. Everything goes wrong. Before it's over you hear yourself yelling things you never intended to say, things that aren't even in the least bit true. Things you'd never say. Things you can never take back.

I want to get it right.

Let me try to give you an example. I've gotten calls from the Highway Patrol at all hours of the night when it's so cold a dog would jump a cat for no reason. So cold I'd have to use ether to get the engine started. I'm hungover sometimes. I leave a warm bed and dress in the dark. If she knows I'm gone, she never says so.

I climb in the cab of my wrecker, and even through the cushion I feel how cold the seat is on the backs of my legs. My breath fills up the whole cab. Sometimes I'm still a little drunk. The gear stick sends an ache through the palm of my hand. When I pull them up from under the seat, my gloves look like chopped off hands. It's that cold. I'm feeling like hell. And I know what I've got to look forward to. I ain't about to get warm. And I'm thinking about what I'm leaving behind. I'm thinking of my wife and the things I don't know how to say to her.

Then heading out east, out to Lamar or Timmonsville there are breaks in the sky, and I know that later the sun will be coming up. I have a cup of Sav-Way coffee. Everything is quiet, the way it is in the South when everything is covered with snow and the moon is full. The blower is hot on my knees now and I can turn it down, too. For a second, I'm not thinking about anything or anybody.

Then I start up a hill and the sky is the color of the ocean just before a storm, gray or bluish, maybe slate colored. Then, at the very top of the hill, the moon is right there, sandwiched between the white land and the sky that's like a tide. And for a second you can't catch your breath, and you're glad as hell to be there, and you feel like the whole thing was planned just for you, or that you've slipped into a moment not meant for a human to see. And you forget about what waits for you eight or ten miles up the road and about what you've left as many miles behind.

There's just you and all this white world around you. It's early in the morning. You're warm, and there's the sky and the moon and the snow everywhere. What I'm trying to say is it's a feeling. That feeling is what I'm trying to say is what true is. It is that feeling, that thing I feel for her, that I can't get across. It all gets lost in the explaining.

I wish I could tell you what it's like at that time in the morning when you come to a flat stretch before the final curve and see the red and blue lights dancing over the snow way up ahead. I feel a little sick, because of what I know way down deep. But at the same time the lights on the snow, red chasing blue, blue chasing red on the ice and snow, and way back the beginnings of the sun and the receding tide of slate sky above, there is a feeling there. Still, I get that churning in my stomach on account of knowing and not knowing for sure what I've got ahead of me.

She says there's something missing.

When I was a boy, before I knew what those lights really meant, I would've sat at the top of the hill and imagined they were lights on a flying saucer or the second coming of Christ. Now I know what it means if the EMS guys are still there when there's snow. It means somebody's dying, dead, or damned near it. Sometimes it means I've got to move some steel before they can finish their work.

I leave the truck running and the blower on high. We, the EMS guys and me, we take turns aiming the lights mounted on the cab and warming our hands. Sometimes we see it, the way people go out of this world. The cold doesn't make it any easier. Sometimes it is so bad that we have to look for bodies thrown from cars. People don't drive as fast in ice and snow, you'd say. But the ice means they don't slow down either.

Sometimes they aren't all there. Parts of them, I mean, are lost.

I don't get paid for helping the guys look. My job is to haul away what's left of the plastic and steel. That's what I get paid for. But I just can't drive away while the others are out there looking. I couldn't do that. I'm not like that. You would think that it didn't matter, not to the dead person. But those EMS guys, they just won't give up looking.

It's what we have in common.

Even when a thing is dead it has its parts, and you owe it to make a broken thing whole, even if you can't give it life again. You and I, we have obligations. We take oaths and say vows. Or at least that's what I think.

I take my turn looking for the parts. Nobody talks. We all know what we have to do, and we know that we have to look close, and we hope that it is somebody else who finally says the search is over.

You would think the parts would be found near the point of impact. You'd be surprised. So you look and you think. Even with the bright lights it is hard to see.

You are always walking in your own shadow.

Sometimes I just want to close my eyes and get down on my hands and knees. Feel for what it is I hope I don't find. I wish I could just come out and tell you. If I had words, I'd tell you.

You can either take people at their word or not. It is a choice. It is a real hard choice. Believing somebody's word takes trust on both sides. It means that one person knows what she is saying and is willing to say it. It means the other person can hear through to the meaning and can take it. Both sides are hard. It comes down to this. When somebody tells you something, they either mean what they say, or they mean something else, or they mean nothing at all. The problem is when they say it straight out. The straighter it is, the harder it is to take sometimes. You would think that the hardest thing would be when someone says, "I don't love you." Worse is when she says, "I love you, but . . . ." It can make you say and do things you'll regret the rest of your life. It'll make you want to get down on your knees.

If the job isn't done when the sun really starts to get up, the EMS guys will go back to the van to warm. Nobody says anything. They just know that in the time it takes them to get warm they'll have the light of the sun to see by.

It's true that it's coldest just before the sun comes up.

They are doing the right thing. If there is anything to be found, waiting a half hour won't make any difference now. Still, after I've been looking I can't go back with the others. They always feel a need to talk.

I can't blame them. I feel it too. People feel uneasy when they are together like that and there is nothing but silence. They feel like there is something they ought to be saying. I understand that. But I can't do it. So I search alone, looking down at the snow, moving slowly, worried I'll bury under my boot the thing I'm looking for. Worried that somehow I already have.

Sometimes after staring down at the snow for a long time in the night, my eyes will play tricks on me. I'll be looking down, and suddenly I'm seeing into nothing at all. I'm not saying this right. I'm seeing the very place where the snow and the night come together, see. I'm looking down from high up and everything just goes down and down, forever. I feel dizzy. I stand very still, and the cold seeps into my bones. I get that numb feeling everywhere. I know I have to bring myself out of it.

So when I feel this way, I sometimes think about the warm place I've left and wish with all my heart I could go back to it, and that it would somehow be there when I get home.

Vibes
Warren and Louise Oxendine

My wife bought a vibrator at a yard sale. It wasn't one of those miniature made-for-Cape-Canaveral shaped ones either. It looked like a power drill. It came with attachments and speed control. She laid it out on the white tablecloth like it was nothing, flanked on one side by a orange Fiesta Ware pitcher, and on the other by a length of pale blue satin. Without so much as a blink, Louise pulled her hair behind her ear, one gray strand falling into a crescent over her eye, and reached inside the brown paper grocery bag again.

"Holy Moly," I said. "Do you know what that thing *is*?" Sometimes Louise would buy yard sale stuff for no other reason than its shape and color. She wouldn't know its name or use. Knickknacks she called them.

She held up six blue, chrome-rimmed coasters in one hand and a roll of red Christmas wrapping paper in the other. "Fifty cents," she said, laying the wrapping paper beside a nutcracker set and the coasters beside the vibrator. I picked it up. It was lighter than it looked.

"Where on earth did you *get* this thing?"

"On mornings like this," she said thoughtfully, "when it looks like rain, that's when you get the best deals." She sifted through the bag. "After people go to the trouble to put everything out, they don't want to pack it up again." She paused, then looked at me for the first time. "The sound of thunder can be a happy sound," she said. Louise spread out several small pieces of glass, spacing them just so.

"What are you going to *do* with this?"

She held up a small prism to the light. "Warren, didn't you say you had a nine o'clock tee time?" she said. The whole spectrum of color crossed her face.

I remember very clearly standing, or leaning rather, in the garage that afternoon with one eye shut counting the remaining woods and irons in my golf bag. I burped about fourteen beers worth and began counting again. Then I stopped counting. Louise's car wasn't parked there where it was supposed to be. I lost count of my clubs and started again. I regretted throwing my sand wedge in the water beside the fourth green, and creating the lightning rod my two wood made in the top of the cypress beside the eighth fairway. I was sorry I'd told Billy Mims to kiss my ass, and that I'd threatened John Truett with my putter after he'd told a joke that I couldn't even remember now. This is a small town, a very small town, and in towns this small, at least in the South, when people behave badly in public, word gets out. People are always watching. And talking. I gave up counting and went inside.

There was a note on the kitchen table. "Decided to get my hair done." I opened another Miller Lite and sat on the sofa. I didn't even turn on the TV. Just stared into the black screen, thinking—listening to the soft sounds of cars passing on the street, waiting for Louise. I can't remember if I finished the beer or not.

I woke when Louise turned on the end table light. I looked up at her, then rubbed my palms into my eyes. I was still a little drunk. She looked different. Her hair had been cut in what she called a wedge. It was dark brown now with a reddish tint in the light. She brought over a sandwich on a tray.

"For what it's worth," she said softly, "just remember, the ball doesn't carry as well in this humidity."

I couldn't get over her hair. The graying had come gradually, never seeming to age her really. But now the cut and the brownish red tint seemed to alter her face altogether, bringing out the angle of her cheeks and the line of her jaw, gifts of her grandmother's Cherokee blood. Her skin seemed darker, richer, the way makeup can never imitate. I just looked at her.

"You'll feel better after you've eaten," she said. She kissed me on the forehead, then turned and walked toward our bedroom. Maybe it was because I was lying on the sofa, or maybe it was the light reflecting off the hardwood floors onto her legs as she walked away, but every curve of her calves was defined by line and shadow, and the skirt gave up an extra inch or two of leg. She was wearing heels. She never wears heels. She closed the door behind her. All the way.

The next morning Louise pulled the covers from my head and gave me a peck on the cheek. "Don't worry, baby, I'll make excuses," she whispered. I didn't open my eyes. "Earl can sing tenor this morning—if he can stay awake during the sermon.".

Call it adolescent perversity if you want, but I peeked out the window and watched her back out of the drive. I went straight to her underwear drawer. I lifted neat stacks of panties and felt around under folded bras, hoping and not hoping that I would feel the cool plastic.

I held up a white nightie that felt like silk, with straps like soft ribbon. I couldn't remember if I had maybe bought it for her years ago and she had never worn it. You know, maybe one Christmas Eve, or one of the days driving home when I remembered all at once it was our anniversary. Bought it without much thought. Then it struck me that maybe I'd never bought it at all, that I'd just seen ones like it in catalogs that came in the mail, that she had maybe bought it for herself and never worn it. The idea of that made me sad. I held it up to my face, brushing over it like a kitten.

Then I thought something else. Maybe *she* hadn't been the one to buy it either. Maybe somebody *else* had bought it for her. I lost control for a minute.

It took me a while to remember what went back into what drawer. I sat huffing for breath, surrounded by the debris of strewn pantyhose, sweaters and underwear. I'd flung empty dresser drawers into every corner of the room. And still, it wasn't there. It occurred to me for the first time, sitting there panting, that I had entered the age when men begin having heart attacks.

I never did get things folded right.

The next Saturday, I begged off the golf game. Billy had been nice about calling again from the course, saying the guys would wait for me if I'd change my mind. In the background I heard John say I could play out of his bag. I felt bad about saying no. They are nice guys and I like playing golf with them, but golf is a mental game. I couldn't afford to give up any more clubs to the water hazards.

I was raising the wheels on the lawn mower when I saw Louise in new sunglasses walking toward me smiling. She was holding two picture frames and her trusty grocery bag of yard sale goodies.

"You won't believe what I bought today," she called. I took a deep breath. She was wearing lipstick. The wind blew her hair back and pressed her thin blouse around her breasts. I could see them rise and gently fall with each step, see the shadow of skin above her bra line rising and falling. The sun was that bright.

"Can't get the wheels back on?" she said, standing over me.

"What do you mean?"

"That look on your face," she said. I couldn't see her eyes behind the sunglasses. She smiled again, extending her hand. "Come on, muscles. I need a *man*." For a second I couldn't find my feet. She led me to the car.

"Call me Bargain Woman," she said.

I helped her get the rowing machine out of the station wagon. It looked brand new. "Fifteen dollars," she said. "We'll put it in Tracy's room." Tracy is our sixteen-year-old. She was spending her summer with a church singing group in Europe.

"I'll enjoy this," she said. We'd set the machine down so that I could catch my breath. "It gives a complete body workout."

"You have to be careful not to overdo it," I said.

"You underestimate me, Warren," she said.

"Let's go out for dinner," I blurted out. "We'll go out for a good steak."

"Really?"

"We'll go to The Steak Barn, maybe have a drink before we eat. You know, make an evening of it."

"I wish you'd told me, baby. I thawed out some chops. They won't be good tomorrow." We set the rower in the bedroom, near the door.

"Okay, how about a movie after dinner."

"Warren? That you?" She put one hand on my forehead, then reached for my wrist. "You hate movies," she said, taking my pulse.

"It's a comedy, though. Josh said he and Rene laughed so hard they cried," I lied. "I really, really want to see it. Really."

"Well, okay. I think you should. I think it would be good for you. Why don't you go to the seven o'clock."

"Whatever you say."

"I can't go, of course."

I pushed aside one of the oars.

"I promised Marie I'd write half the invitations for your niece's shower, you know."

"That won't take all night, will it?"

"Noooo," she said, letting the "O" ring. Neither of us said anything. "You go to the movie, baby. I can amuse myself if I try hard." She patted my hand. "You are sweet to ask though."

All through dinner I told Louise I wasn't going to the movie. I told her my stomach hurt, which was true. I have an ulcer. That's all the more reason why I should go, why a good laugh would be good for me, she said. I was still refusing when she handed me my car keys and closed the door behind me. I heard the door lock. I rang the doorbell.

"You locked the door," I said when she opened it. "Why did you lock the door?"

She just looked at me for a second. Like I was crazy.

"Would you rather I didn't, big boy," she said in a real sexy voice, suddenly caressing the door frame, for god's sake, smiling. I really didn't like the way she smiled. It seemed to say about ten things at once. "Well, would you?"

What could I say? I felt like a fool.

She became herself again. "You have a good time," she said, giving me a full body hug. She smiled with a kind of universal understanding. I felt ashamed.

"We have to take care of ourselves," she said, a slight lilt in her voice. I was out of the drive before it occurred to me she was wearing a perfume I didn't remember smelling before.

I didn't laugh once. Not through the whole first half of the movie. I had got to thinking. I left my seat and started the climb toward the exit of the dark theater. Just as I reached the door, the whole damned room exploded in laughter. I took a deep breath and left the theater.

I stopped at The Paradise Lounge for a couple of bourbons, which I watched turn to water on the bar, but still I was home by 9:30. I saw the invitations on the kitchen table, and the pen. But I didn't see any *written* invitations anywhere. The house was silent.

"Louise?" I said softly. There was no answer. I listened, walking cautiously back toward our bedroom. Her breathing was slow but hard, as if she were holding her breath in between, like a swimmer or something. I stopped in the hall, listening.

I thought I'd go back to the kitchen and drop a glass or something. I slipped out of my shoes.

Then I thought maybe I'd go outside and ring the doorbell. I tiptoed toward the bedroom door. Her breathing was really hard, a real throaty breathing like I'd never heard.

I've always believed in people's privacy. I crept nearer the door.

I won't call it a moan, but it was a voicey sound. Followed by the sound of movement in the bed. I took a deep breath and held it. Then I peeked around the door. She was on her back, eyes closed, her mouth slightly open—snoring.

Never in seventeen years of marriage had she ever snored. She had complained for as long as I could remember that she was a light sleeper. I couldn't tell you what time she usually went to sleep, but sometimes after midnight when I woke to go to the bathroom she would still be reading. I can tell you that much. She didn't even budge when I

crawled in beside her. She was that deeply asleep.
     I looked at the clock. It said quarter to ten.

     She said, "I'm going shopping, honey." And I said, "Okay,
dear."
     This time I started searching in the guest bedroom.
     Nothing.

     A week later, I came home early from work. I'm in the insurance
business. Risk analysis. I wanted to have a talk with Louise. On the
way in that morning, I'd begun thinking about where I might search next,
where I hadn't already looked. I couldn't keep my mind on my work.
Couldn't concentrate at all. Then I said to myself, well Warren, what are
you gonna do when you do find the damned thing?
     On the way home, I thought about a lot of things and none of
them were good. For starters, I pictured Louise talking sweetly to her
vibrator while packing my bags. Then I thought of something even
worse, that maybe there was another man who had introduced her to
things I'd never dreamed of. And that she liked it. I drove through a stop
sign I've known for thirty years.
     When I looked at myself in the rearview mirror, my face was so
red I thought a vein might burst somewhere.
     But by the time I parked in the drive, I felt like a creep for
thinking what I had. I didn't want to get out of the car and face Louise,
who had never been anything but kind and faithful. I unconsciously
reached up to my shirt pocket for a cigarette. I'd quit six years before
when the doctor had given the warning about my heart. He'd said I'd
better take it easy. I'd taken it easy all right. My wife had bought a
vibrator at a yard sale. I made myself get out of the car and go inside.
     This time it wasn't snoring. Not this time. The sounds were
unmistakable to my mind, sounds I'd never heard but unmistakable
nevertheless. There were these—it sounds ugly but it's true—these
grunting sounds, these little cries, followed by long "uhhhhhhhh" sounds
that broke off abruptly. Then the series began again, building to a gasp,
a final thrusting "uh!" Even before I got to the bedroom door I could
feel even the floor moving. It was moving, no doubt. I laid my ear to the

door. It was undeniable. There was a low humming. The little cries, "Uh, Uh, Uh, Uh," were louder, faster. I felt my face getting red again. I shoved the door open.

My first thoughts were that I was dying. It was the eruption of bells, I suppose, that occurred the second I pushed the door open. Then I realized the ringing came from the timer in Louise's hand. She sat on the rower in silver and black tights that looked like spray paint. She was wearing a red headband.

"My, that was a good workout," she said, catching her breath, looking down at the timer. After a second or two she looked up. "What are you doing home early? Warren, do you feel all right?"

"Louise," I said. Then I didn't know what to say. I stood there. A little half smile appeared on her face.

She held her hand up to me, and I took it. She stood and led me down the hall to our bedroom. "I thought I'd get out of these tights," she said. She drew the curtains and pulled back the covers.

She didn't make one single little crying sound. She didn't even breathe hard once.

"Don't forget your Men's Club meeting tonight," she said a little later. She was staring at the ceiling. "I want you to go. I've run out of excuses at church. I've got to get the pot roast in the oven."

Then she was out of bed. I heard the shower. I hadn't showered with her in years, I thought. Not that she had seemed to mind. It wasn't as if she'd asked and I'd refused or anything.

After a couple of minutes I had the strength to sit up. I rose slowly and walked naked into the bath. Seeing her through the glass shower door, Louise looked like a painting. She stood motionless, her arms up, hands holding her hair, her head arched way back under the spray. I'd never seen her like that before, or not for a very, very long time. It was like a new memory, if that makes sense. Out of nowhere I thought I might cry. I reached for a bath cloth. I looked at myself in the mirror. I turned around and walked out.

It took me a long time to get to sleep that night. I had dreams that I was glad I couldn't remember. But in the morning I was left with a single undeniable impression: It had to be somewhere in that house.

I can't tell you how I ended up in the attic. I started in the kitchen with the china cabinet, and moved to the canned foods. At some point my hand was feeling around in the bottom of the flour bin. Then, I was standing in the attic, surrounded by the accumulation of my life. I stopped to catch my breath. The plywood floor formed an island in the center of the large attic. Insulation, like pink snow, circled the stacks of boxes. Everything was covered in dust. There were boxes everywhere, some overflowing with old clothes and dishes. A brown cardboard suitcase spilled over with black and white photographs. A fruit crate held a stack of wrinkled record albums. Bobby Vinton smiled a twisted smile through the gray haze. "Blue Velvet." "The Limbo Game." Sam Cooke's wife shot him. Or was it somebody else? One box was filled with naked Barbies and Kens. There were feet in the air, arms and hands everywhere. I stepped on a Christmas tree ball, leaving a halo of blue and red glitter on the plywood.

Some of the boxes were collections of Louise's yard sale finds. One small box was filled with red, blue, green, and yellow aluminum glasses from the 50's. Farther back was a box filled with very old green antique glass figures and vases. There was another one marked "collectibles." Magazines and old newspapers spewed from others.

Then I saw the metal detector. My heart leapt.

I'd bought it about fifteen years earlier, when they'd first hit the market, and taken it to the beach once or twice. But in those days I had been too fond of bikinis to keep my eyes on the sand. A clean sweep line is very important if you're serious about your detecting work. I'd found a wedding band one time. I didn't know if it would detect batteries. I knew it would work through plastic though.

The earphones were hard as oak; the rubber seemed to have petrified. But the meter still worked. I ran my left hand, my wedding band, under the circular face of the metal detector. I heard the beep. The needle on the meter pointed to gold. Beginning in the back right corner of the plywood platform, I swept for mines. In one box I found maybe twenty silver candleholders. After searching through its contents, I moved on. In another, I found hundreds of antique earrings, bracelets, and silver plated compacts. Soon, the room was a haze of dust. My eyes watered, I coughed and sputtered. I had to stop for a sneezing fit.

My ears really hurt. Time to give up, I thought. Near the door, I picked up the flashlight I'd put there years ago for Louise. The batteries were as strong as ever. I aimed its beam through the smoky dust all around the room, out to the regions below low rafters.

Then I saw the box. It was near the door, little more than ten feet from where I'd entered, but way back under the eve of the roof. It was a new box. The words "Thigh Master" were printed on the outside in blue letters. But in Magic Marker, written in Louise's hand, were the words "My Toys." Thigh Master Toys, I thought.

I'd only taken two steps across the beams when my foot slipped on the dust-slick two-by-fours. Why the ceiling didn't give way I'll never know. I stepped back. I sneezed three times and rubbed my eyes. I assessed the risk. I looked again at the toy box.

I moved my old skis to sit down and think. I thought.

I hadn't been snow skiing in years, but I got the skis on easily enough. I wiped the dust from an old diving mask and pulled it over my eyes. I lifted the metal detector, adjusted the painful earphones, took a deep breath, and began gliding over the rafters and pink snow. I moved with ease, skis secure, eyes clear behind the thin plastic, metal detector swinging gracefully. I felt like I was under water or on the moon, nearing the wreck, anticipating and yet fearing what I might find. I ran the detector over the box. My ears rang. I used the lip of the detector like a snake probe to open the lid. I could hear my heart beating in my ears. Music boxes. Louise's music boxes.

"Warren? My God, Warren. That you, Warren?" When I turned, she started laughing. She didn't stop. The least she could have done was go on back down stairs. But she didn't. She held her side and wiped the tears from her eyes and looked at me, top to bottom, up and down, mask to skis. I took off the headphones and dropped the metal detector right there. Louise was howling.

"Oh God, Warren, where *is* the camera. Oh Warren, Warren, this is priceless. Don't move."

I jerked away the mask, slam-dunked it into the pink insulation. I could feel its red outline over my cheeks and on my forehead.

"I just want to know one thing, Louise," I shouted. I was really angry now. "One thing." She was laughing so hard she was making little wheezing sounds. Slowly, I lifted the skis and slammed them down Cro-Magnon on the rafters. Every clumsy step sent her into new regions of lunatic ecstasy.

"I just want to know this," I said, making my way back toward her, trying to make myself heard.

"Forget about our plans for Switzerland," she said in a sort of little girl squeal. She was crying laughing tears.

I was closing in on her. She started to back away a little. "I want to know why you bought that vibrator."

She doubled over. She wasn't even making laughing sounds

now. Her whole body was convulsing. She looked up, holding up one hand like a traffic cop as if to say, no more, no more.

"And I want to know NOW!" I slammed down a ski for added emphasis.

"Because," she began, and then made little seal noises, "arf, arf, arf, arf," catching her breath. "Because the woman I bought it from— said—it—had never been—used. That's why." She was howling again, backing down the stairs.

"Never been USED! Name for me somebody who got a toy and didn't *play* with it." She was out of sight. I dropped on my side, rolled over on my stomach, and holding up the skis like TV antennas, slid on my chest to the stair opening. I plunged my head down. Blood rushed. She staggered out of sight.

"Think of nuclear weapons, for God's sake," I shouted. "We even had to try those out. How on earth can you expect me to . . ." Then she was in the other room, our bedroom, just below me. I could tell from her laughing.

That night in bed I thought she was asleep, but she wasn't. "I realized something in the attic today," she said in the darkness.

"I don't even want to know," I said.

She didn't say anything else, but I could feel the bed vibrating from her restrained laughter.

Sometime later just before I went to sleep she whispered, "I love you, Warren."

Louise was gone when I woke up. I laid my arm over to where she always sleeps. Old habits die hard. The sheets were cold. But her clothes were still hanging in the closet. I looked out the window. The station wagon was still in the garage. Downstairs, she'd left a note on the kitchen table. It said, "Warren, this is serious. Meet me in the attic when you get home from work. I'll be there. No joke."

I showered and dressed in a daze. While waiting for the light at the intersection of Hawthorne and Miller, Louise, in black and silver tights and red nylon shorts, jogged in front of my car. She was looking up at the light, wearing Walkman headphones. And making pretty good time.

I'm not really as square as most people think. I mean, I'm not opposed to trying new things. Louise and I had had our experimental phase the first year we were married. There is nothing unusual about that. And just for the record, I'd been the one to take the lead. We'd even done it in the car once. At home we'd done it in every room at one time or another. I'm not really the athletic type, but I've had my moves. The attic never counted as a room before.

At work, I closed the door to my office and took the phone off the hook. I sat. For the first time I visualized Louise with the thing. But the woman wasn't really Louise somehow. It became one of those sex movies.

The line to Pastor Ferkin's office was busy. We'd been friends for years, although church business was our only connection. He conducted marriage seminars. He took college courses. I was sure he'd heard it all. I tried again. The phone rang on the other end. He said hello. I hung up the receiver.

I called home. I kept calling home.

When I walked in the door, I saw the attic stairs had been pulled down.

"Louise? Louise, I'm home." I sounded like a TV Dad from the fifties.

"Warren? Oh, Warren, come quick," came the voice upstairs. "I want you to see this, Warren. Hurry."

I took the steps slowly. My head went up like a periscope. Louise sat cross-legged, her back to me. At the head of the steps, I saw that she was hunched over a brown suitcase filled with old photographs.

"Look, look at this." She was holding a snapshot. In it we sat on a blanket at the beach, the first summer we dated. We were looking into the camera—our arms interlocked champagne fashion, feeding each other ice cream. Ice cream was all over our mouths. She smiled up at me and gave me a little kiss.

"This is the plan," she said, laying the photo aside. "I've priced most everything in this firetrap with these stickers." She lifted a small lamp from a box, pointed at its sticker. "Help me get the stuff down stairs. I can get it out on the lawn by myself in the morning. You can sleep until I get really busy. Did you see the signs?"

"What signs?"

"My yard sale signs, you bat-blind bad boy."

I stood on the steps and took the boxes from Louise. There were at least twice as many as I would have guessed were up there. Together we stacked them in the living room.

"Could we maybe have that romantic steak dinner tonight?" she purred.

I was dead asleep. It was pitch dark.

"Wake up, Warren. I have everything out, but it feels like rain outside. They're here already." She'd left a cup of coffee beside the bed.

I looked out the window as I dressed. The sky was pink in the east, black in the north. Louise, in brown slacks and a blue blouse, scurried from customer to customer haggling over prices, making yard sale magic. I poured a second cup of coffee for myself and one for Louise. I still had sleep in my eyes when I walked outside.

"You're in charge of the strongbox," she said, pointing to my green tackle box. "They'll bring you the stickers. You make change."

Louise seemed to float over the lawn, sidestepping old ladies holding up curtains, pirouetting past professional junk shop men, gliding over an old Hoover pulled like a pet by a little girl. At one point she began singing "We're in the money," holding up maybe fifteen one-dollar bills. She threw her arm around my neck, and I joined in the chorus. She sang alto. I sang tenor. People looked at us and smiled.

About eight-thirty everybody stopped dead still. A long roll of thunder crossed overhead.

"Everything half price," she announced. "Everything's got to go." I took in quarters and dimes, and folded warm dollars that appeared from between melon-sized breasts.

Louise said the word would be out in thirty minutes. And sure enough in half an hour there must have been fifty people in our yard. At times, I couldn't see over the circle that surrounded me, people shoving stickers at me. One guy asked if the ladder in my garage was for sale.

I couldn't believe what people would buy. There was absolutely no logic to the sales. I'd try to guess what would sell next and who would buy it. Not once was I right.

Then the swarm was gone. The wave had passed. Two young women who had driven up in a red Volvo were going through baby clothes Louise had kept for fourteen years. Another woman was holding up an old bra.

"Can I get you another cup of coffee," I called to Louise.

"Oh yes, please," she said.

I poured our coffee, but I couldn't remember which cup had sugar. Louise likes sugar. I take mine black. I lifted a cup and tasted.

From the kitchen window, I watched Louise refolding drapes and old jeans. She looked happy.

For the first time, I realized that yard sale crazies, as Louise referred to herself, were really lovers of mystery and surprise. They were optimists. They were discoverers. They sometimes didn't know what would please them until they saw it. They didn't over-value things. They were willing to compromise. They believed there was something waiting for them out there. I topped off my cup.

I heard a peal of laughter outside. Louise and the two women who'd driven up in the Volvo were looking into a small red and black rectangular box, laughing. By the time I got outside, the women were driving away.

"What was so funny," I said. Louise was waving to them as they pulled away. She was still laughing though.

"Oh, nothing," she said, "yard sale talk." Smiling to herself, she looked over at a middle-aged woman and her husband. The wife rummaged through knickknacks. The husband waited for her, checking his watch every minute or two. "May I help you?" Louise said. The woman looked up and smiled.

"Maybe," she said.

"I'll wait for you in the car, babydoll," the husband said. He gave her a little peck on the cheek and turned toward the street.

"I'll only be a minute," she said. "I promise."

"Take your time," he said. "I'll listen to the radio."

"I've just the thing for you," Louise said, taking the woman by the arm, watching the husband walk away. She stopped and looked at me. "Warren, would you be a sweetheart and go inside and get me a cup of coffee?" Louise led the woman toward a half-empty cardboard box under a table.

Her cup was full, the coffee still warm. I carried it inside to the kitchen and emptied the coffee down the drain. I walked slowly from room to room, looked at the photographs of our small family on the walls and tables, ran my fingers over the soft linens on our bed before circling back to the kitchen. Then without looking out the window I poured the last of the coffee into Louise's cup, measured a level teaspoon of sugar, and then stirred it slowly, until I thought it was just right.

Gatsby's Last Dive
Giles Carter

The impossible is what he had trouble with. You can see him now in his Calvin Klein swimsuit, toes at the very edge of the curved tile, looking down at his own distorted image in the blue-green water, lamenting every blade of grass that mars its perfect, tiny waves, listening as the water softly collides with the tiles—sounding vaguely like kisses he had known. He should never have put it to her that way. There must have been a hundred ways he could have gotten around to it, ways that she could have told him what he needed to hear, ways that could have been easy for her.

But he misunderstood so many things. Mostly he misunderstood the nature of love, its paradoxes, or at least its ironies. And that's why things turned out okay for him in the end. Because thanks to a grease monkey with a .45, he didn't have to face up to those complexities. He had a grease monkey do it for him. The grease monkey was highly conflicted. Or maybe not. Maybe he was a grease monkey without his own swimming pool. If not for the grease monkey, the one who did him a favor by greasing him, he would have had to face up to so many things. Like the fact that she did love him, but that she realized—where he didn't—that fate is prescriptive. She could see it coming; he couldn't. He would've had to face up to the fact that she knew love was not a thing to run to, finally.

In the end, the need for safety always exceeds the need for love. It would have ruined him had he actually learned that, come to know it in a way he couldn't shake it. Much better to take a swim, to lie there thinking about how to make it go, to contemplate the next move.

His fatal mistake was not believing her when she didn't say it. She could say it to him, all right. She could say it to him and mean it. Say it truthfully. With all her heart. Because she did love him. But his mistake was in what he mistook for love. Fact is, she was right and he was wrong. She gets safety, the only substitute for love; he gets a fish-eye view of the pool drain through hazy green water.

His last swim, though, was not his worst day. His worst day was when he forced the issue, when he said that she must say to her husband that she'd never loved him—as he, Gatsby, witnessed the telling. Had he been able to envision her saying it to the hubby, perhaps he could have settled for that. But his was a failure of the imagination. And he had envisioned so much.

You can picture him floating there, knowing that somehow, some way, he can fix it. He knows there are ways to convert old currency into new currency. Cunning and dedication are what is needed. With love he can't lose. You can picture him, following his dream into sleep, the water all around him, his body conforming to subtle currents, the low sun turning his blue-green pallet into a dazzling bed of yellow glitter.

You can see him there as the barrel of the pistol enters the frame. And you wait with deep longing, with envy and delight.

Wheels
Harman and Charlene Parnell

Harman Parnell had been out of work for nine months when he took the job selling mobile homes. He told the mall store manager at Sears, where he'd sold tires before that, to kiss his ass. It had been coming for a long time. He felt good saying it.

Everything since then had been downhill.

If his wife, Charlene, hadn't pressured him, he would have given up after so many months of looking. Just get something temporary, she said. It doesn't have to be much. Think of it as insulation she said. His wife, who worked at Faith Bread Nursing Home, said he should be glad he had work again selling trailers, said he didn't know how hard it had been for her to support them both. Everything's temporary, she'd say. Harman didn't think of it that way. After nearly a year at Winner's World Mobile Homes, he still found that the first thing he looked at when a semi pulled onto the lot were its tires.

Charlene had peeled down her panty hose to her ankles when Harman walked in from work. She sat on the very edge of the sofa leaning toward the TV screen, as if it sucked her forward. "Things keep getting more and more miserable," she said, not looking up at Harman. She lifted her feet and peeled off the hose one foot at a time. Harman went into the kitchen and came back with two tall Budweisers. He handed her one.

On the screen a woman with a face like a man's mopped her tears with a Kleenex. The camera cut to Jerry Springer, who stood solemnly, head down.

"What's this about?" Harman said, opening his beer.

"I don't know," Charlene said, slowly nodding. "I just don't know." A commercial featuring an infant cradled in a car tire appeared on the screen. They watched.

Charlene took a long drink. "These panty hose cut off my circulation," she said, not taking her eyes from the set. "I'm getting fat."

"What's that?" Harman said, nodding toward the set.

On the screen, Jerry squinted one eye, tilting his head away from the man who sat beside the crying woman, the woman with the face of a man. Everybody in the audience was waiting, waiting for him to say something, waiting like a lynch mob. You could see it on their faces.

Later Harman and Charlene sat at the kitchen table. It was dark outside. Somehow a cricket had got in the house. They sat listening.

Harman couldn't see where the noise was coming from. He looked over at the heap of dishes in the sink.

"Let's not cook tonight," he said.

"Okay," she said. "We'll go out."

"Let's go out someplace nice. I finally got commission today."

"We've got bills," she said.

"It's up to you," he said.

"Let's think," she said, getting beers. She sat down again, and they opened the beers. "Oh, where do you want to go?"

"Do you want to just do this," he said, lifting his beer, "or not?" He looked over at her. She seemed to be looking at something far away. "Do you want to go out or not?"

"I'll have to get dressed," she said.

Entertainment World was the name of the show Harman was watching.

"What should I wear?" Charlene called from the other room.

"Whatever," Harman called back. The portion of the show he was watching was about an old movie, one about a murderer who ate his victims after killing them. Ate them down to their bones.

Charlene shouted over the TV from the other room. "I've got this blue one, or this red jumper. Where are we going, anyway?" She waited a second. "How fancy do you want to go?"

Harman tried hard to hear the set. The character in the movie, Hannibal the Cannibal, was leaning into the camera, close up, whispering. Harman couldn't make out the secret in the guy's voice.

Again, from the other room: "I look good in this black one, but you'll have to take me someplace nice or I'll definitely be overdressed. People will stare."

Harman moved closer to the set.

"You're not even listening, are you?" she said from the other room. "Are you?"

"Just wear your panties and bra," Harman shouted. He'd missed it. The baby-in-the-tire commercial came on again. He hit the power button. Hannibal was sucked into the darkness. "Just let's get going."

Charlene appeared in the doorway in her black bra and panties, smiling past him with distant, shiny eyes. She lifted her beer, rested her shoulder against the doorframe. She was thinking of herself in a sexy movie. Harman could see the leftover line of the pantyhose that divided her in half.

"On second thought," he said, "wear the blue one."

Her eyes returned from wherever they had been. She looked down at herself.

"Only don't wear any underwear," Harman said quickly, attempting to reverse gravity. He was sorry for what he'd said. Sorry the second he heard it come out.

She turned.

"You fuck, you," she said.

When they sat in the Mustang to leave, Harman told her he'd like to take her kids to the beach on Sunday. He meant it this time. Charlene, seven years older than Harman, had had the first one when she was nineteen. She'd given up the kids to get the divorce the quickest way. Both the boy and the girl were in high school now. Both hated Harman. They lived with their father. We'll take a picnic, Harman said. That would be nice, Charlene said, moving close beside him. He felt in his jacket, but his keys weren't there.

"I ought to turn the porch light on," she said, looking back at the small, faceless house.

"Unless you want to eat pancakes, we better get going." He patted his trouser pocket.

"I hate coming home to a dark house."

"I'll get it," Harman said, a little agitated at not finding the keys.

"No, I'll get it," she said, taking out her keys. "I'll get the light."

"No," he said. "Give me the keys. I'll get the light. It's too damp for you to be walking out here in heels. You might break something."

"Really, I don't mind," she said, opening her door.

He just looked at her. "Give me the damn keys." Then he got out of the car and started toward the house.

Charlene's eyes were drawn to the wrecked and abandoned cars that surrounded the old garage behind their house. The cars' dead headlights reflected the moonlight like crowded marble headstones.

Harman unlocked the door, reached inside, and found the light switch. Walking back, he glanced over his shoulder. The house wasn't much, but at least it hadn't arrived on wheels. He'd seen what fire could do. Sometimes all that was left were the tires, and the disclaimers.

"Disclaimers," he could hear Ransom Fields, his boss at Winner's World, say. "A contract is only as good as its disclaimers. In this business disclaimers mean everything" – he'd pause to let it soak in–"if you want to *survive*." When you come to know things, Harman thought, you can't not know them.

"I would have done it," Charlene said when he got back in the car. "I would have cut on the light." She opened beers and began pouring them into Atlanta Braves beer cups. "It's just spooky without a light at night."

Harman always took the back way to Hartsville when he was drinking. The last time he got caught, the judge had been very explicit.

They drove past hundred acre fields of cotton that looked like ragged snow under the fall moon, took the split at the furniture stripping shop, and passed the church that had been spray painted with black swastikas and fuck you's in the spring. The paint had been removed, but you could still see everything.

Ransom, the owner of Winner's World, had a saying. Born for the business. Harman, Ransom said the day he hired him, was born for the business. He told Harman not to worry. There was no such thing as bad times in the mobile home business. Insulation, he called it. "It's on account of the economy," he'd said. "When times are like they are now, people can't afford anything else. When times turn good, you always got the horneymoaners." Horneymoaners were young kids, high school or just out, whose parents couldn't convince them not to get married, who couldn't get across that they had no future. He said Harman was born for the business. Today he'd made commission.

"If we were driving to California, I wonder how many states we'd cross before you'd talk to me," Charlene said.

"You're some conversationalist," Harman said. He looked in his mirror. He saw headlights. He looked down, concentrating, holding the speedometer at 57.

"You're right," Charlene said. "That's not much of an invitation to talk, is it?" She pressed herself against him, lit a cigarette, and held it up to his lips. "Wanna share?" she said in her sexy voice. "I do." She rested a hand on the inside of his thigh.

The car behind him was closer now, its highbeams like lasers. They close in on you, Harman thought, get dangerously close, make you drive too fast or too slow or cross the line. Then they nail you.

Charlene waited. The smoke mushroomed around Harman's head. Finally, she reached over and took the cigarette from Harman's lips, sighed audibly, then brought it to her own lips, taking a long slow pull, looking straight ahead. "You're some salesman," Charlene said, looking away from him, out at the dead, black tobacco stalks, blowing out the smoke with every word, "some salesman all right."

Born for the business, Ransom said, was hustling. You got to *hustle*, he'd say, leaning in, letting his glasses slide down, aiming his good eye over the designer frames, pausing for the effect to take hold. The Big Guy always wore pink tinted glasses when he dealt with customers or did the TV commercials, but he took them off around the salesmen, especially when he was saying more than he was saying. The blind eye was sky blue and looked like it'd just come out of a freezer.

Harman glanced into his mirror, into blinding fog lights at his bumper. He could feel the hard light pressing against the back of his head. The car took the other lane. He gripped the wheel. Music preceded it as the driver pulled up beside him. A kind of chant and booming thud thumped against his window. The car cut over into the lane in front of him. Harman hit the high beams. But the car, a Firebird with black windows and a Show House bumper sticker, raced out of sight, its taillights dissolving red eyes.

"Remember when you used to sing to me?" she said.

"That what you want? Me to sing for it?"

"Married people play games," she said. "That's how they keep it interesting."

When they pulled into the parking lot of The Dragon Inn, there was only a white ragtop Cadillac and a dirty station wagon in the lot. Everything inside was red, except the black booths and the enormous gold dragon that stretched the length of the wall. It had pointed, flickering electric light bulbs for eyes. There were red candles in red glasses on every table.

A teenage couple sat in the back booth facing them. The guy had a long tooth earring that Harman could see from the door. At a booth on the other side were the tops of four heads under a cloud of cigarette smoke. There was nobody at the cash register.

"Don't tell me they're closed already," Charlene said in a little girl's voice.

Harman looked over into a dark corner at the waiter who was talking on the pay telephone. The waiter, a lanky, sandy haired kid in a red jacket, turned his back when Harman spotted him.

"It's not ten o'clock yet, is it? Look at your watch, Harman. The sign said open till ten. It can't be ten yet."

The waiter crushed out his cigarette on the telephone box, then stuffed the butt in the change return. He hung up and trudged past Harman and Charlene, scooping up two menus.

Charlene slid into the booth, smiled up at him, and patted the seat beside her. Harman waited for the four men who had been in the far booth to pass. Two of them had their wallets out. Then he sat beside Charlene. The waiter brought water and took out a small, white pad. Looking back at the teenagers, he reached in his red jacket for a pen. Charlene held the wine list. "Let's have a drink before dinner," she said.

From the register, the fat one with his wallet out called to the waiter in a singsongy voice. "Your tip is shrinking," he said.

"Yours is too, hotshot," said the thin one with the diamond on his index finger to the fat one. The other men laughed in collusion. Charlene was still studying the wine list.

Squeezing the white pad in his palm, the waiter looked down at Charlene. "I'll be back in a minute," he said.

"What's a Kamikaze?" Charlene said to Harman.

"It's different liquors. It's strong."

"Can we have one?"

Before they'd finished their drink, the two teenagers got up from the far booth. Watching them, Harman could feel the drink working on him, making the couple a little fuzzy in his eyes. They were dressed identically, black boots and jeans, black tee shirt and a faded denim jacket. When they got close Harman could see the girl's nipples.

"Hornymoaners," Charlene said, a little too loud, smiling at Harman.

The waiter came back to the table. "Ready now?" he said. Charlene put her arm around Harman, kissed his ear with her tongue, and looked up at the waiter.

"Give us a minute," Harman said, picking up a menu and moving away from Charlene.

"May take longer than a minute, darlin'," Charlene said to the waiter.

When the waiter passed through the kitchen door, he pushed it hard enough to bang the back wall.

"What do you want," Harman said. "We ought to eat something now."

"What I want ain't on the menu," Charlene purred.

"Knock it off," said Harman. "It's late. What do you want?"

Charlene took the menu from him and pushed it across the table. "Kiss me," she said. "Come on. Nobody's here. Come on. Even if you don't mean it. You didn't love every girl you ever kissed, did ya?"

The kitchen door swung open, and the waiter marched out. Behind him a short, bulldog-faced cook wrung his hands in his dirty apron.

"Kitchen closes in fifteen minutes," the young waiter said, not looking up from the pad in his hand. "What'll it be?"

"Hornymoaners," Charlene said looking at Harman, smiling but not smiling.

Looking at the menu, Harman lifted his hand and stroked her hair. "What would you like?" he said.

"I don't know. Sell me something."

"We'll gct two things and share," he said.

"That would be nice," she said, smiling. "I'll eat some of yours and you can eat some of mine."

The waiter sighed and rolled his eyes. Harman looked up at him hard. "Buzz off, asshole," he said. Charlene put her hand on his leg.

"Okay," he said after the waiter had left. He wouldn't look up from the menu. "What will it be?"

"You *could* order for us, if you *wanted* to." She moved her hand up, watching his reaction.

"This is our goddamn night out," he said, pushing her away harder than he had intended. "This is our goddamn night out. What do you want?"

"Hornymoaners," she said again.

"I'm ordering," he said.

"Let's pretend we're someplace else. Some other planet. We just met." She finished her drink. "You're like a salesman, and we just left some Martian hotel bar."

"I'm ordering now."

"Martian man of action."

The waiter pretended he didn't see Harman signal for him, then stood four feet away holding his pad, looking up at the yellow acoustic tile.

"We'll have the chicken and the beef," Harman said, pointing at the menu.

"No, not the chicken. I don't like the chicken."

"What do you want then?"

Charlene began to study the menu. The waiter walked over to the head of the dragon. He screwed the flickering eyes in and out.

"Try to sell me the chicken."

Harman jerked the menu from her hands.

"Maybe some pork and seafood," Charlene said.

"You don't want the beef?"

"I love the beef, Mr. Sales Commission. The more beef the

better. *Definitely* the beef."

"But not the chicken."

"No, the pork or seafood or whatever."

"You want the pork and seafood?"

"Pork, beef, seafood, whatever."

"Name it."

"It doesn't matter."

"Name it."

"Some salesman you are."

"Name it."

"Horneymoaners."

Everything shrill. Everything white.

Charlene felt the back of her head slam against the wall. Harman's fingers pulled at the back of her hair until her eyes looked like a marble statue's. He pressed his body against her. She tried to scream, but it came out as only hot breath on his face.

"I'm calling the police, I'm calling the police!" the young waiter shouted. The bulldog face of the cook hung open in disbelief. Harman was pressing hard against her. He felt Charlene's breasts rising and falling. He could feel the contracting heart squeezing blood through her.

They were in the Mustang driving, Charlene sobbing and moaning. He reached over for her, but she squeezed her fists into balls. She looked away from him out the window. He tuned the radio to soft music.

After a time he reached for her again. She moved beside him, laying her head on his shoulder, crying softly. At a stoplight, Harman turned to see a couple, the girl in a cheerleader dress, looking over at him and Charlene, whose head still lay on his shoulder. Both kids smiled.

Harman drove to the edge of town. At the last street light he turned the car around. He drove back in the direction of the square, the block around the courthouse where the kids circled with their dates. Charlene wasn't crying. Harman thought she was sleeping.

Across the bridge, Harman spotted the circle of light that was the high school football stadium.

"What is it?" Charlene said. "What is it?"

"Looks like a spaceship or something, doesn't it?"

"I wish it was." She sat up, looking away from him out her window at the receding bed of white light. "I wish it was."

They didn't talk.

Harman signaled, then turned onto the square and fell in the procession of kids from the game whose cars formed a chain that crept around and around the center of town. They followed the kids.

"Where are we going?" she asked softly.

"To eat, you mean?"

"You don't know where we're going," she said. "You don't have a clue. You don't have the slightest idea where we're headed. You don't know shit."

Harman didn't say anything. The cars stopped and started. The brake lights lit up in red synchronicity as cars entered or left the circle. The faces of driver and passenger were bathed in the red light.

Harman didn't say anything. They came to a complete stop.

He just waited for her to say it again.

Grits
Charlene and Harman Parnell

Charlene Parnell sits on her sofa dripping hot grits from a spoon into Harman's ear. Harman's head rests on Charlene's lap. The ear canal overflows, and Charlene sees the famous castle at the Magic Kingdom take shape in her mind. The steaming grits are white, not yellow grits. Yellow for corn bread, she thinks, but you want your grits from white corn. The spoon she holds is silver, engraved with a swastika, one her father brought back from Berlin, one her mother fed her from. Over the years, Charlene has polished the spoon and returned it to its small brown box lined with crushed, faded paper, which is as soft as satin from age and smells like the nursing home where she works. She had been saving the spoon for the baby Harman promised when she left her first husband.

Charlene holds the spoon with the steady hand of a surgeon, at a height and angle to create a perfect thin line of white smoke. Like drawing with a long, sharp, invisible pencil. Harman feels nothing.

An instant panic surges through her. A violent, explosive moment in *The Terminator*, Harman's favorite video, suddenly blasts from the TV positioned on the bar separating the kitchen from the living room. Harman had counted the number of times he and Charlene had seen the video, but Charlene will never know the exact number. She presses the mute button. Harman can't add this one to his list.

"The perfect ending to a perfect evening," he had boasted earlier, entering the kitchen holding the cassette box like a trophy. The hour before, after five Kamikazes, Harman had reached for the Mustang keys and proclaimed it Terminator Time, leaving Charlene standing at her mirror holding a tube of lipstick.

"A lot was riding on this evening," Charlene said when Harman returned, not looking up from the soapy dishwater.

"A lotta riding this evening is right," Harman answered back, humping the side of her hip.

The muted screen fills with fire and smoke and flying glass; the spoon above Harman's ear floats suspended in space, the creamy grits smoking. Charlene looks again at the tiny volcano rising from what once was Harman's ear and thinks now of the dripping sand castles she built as a child at Myrtle Beach. She can smell the brackish air.

The childhood memory is shattered when Charlene hears an unfamiliar sound outside. It is the sound of metal against concrete, and it comes from out back in Harman's garage. She listens. She looks at the clock. It is nearly eleven. She reaches for the remote and terminates the video.

Taking a patch of his hair in her left hand and sliding her right hand under his heavy jaw, Charlene concentrates on the grits castle and prepares to lift Harman's head from her lap. The head feels as heavy as a bowling ball. She lifts it, careful not to disturb her work, and tries to slide her bottom to the side. But she wears no panties under her black and white polka-dotted mini-skirt. Her thighs and buttocks are stuck to the black Naugahyde. Again she hears the scraping sound of metal on concrete outside.

Charlene peels her legs from the sofa. With her left hand, she reaches for the pillow Harman's mother embroidered as a wedding gift. She pauses as the faint smell of her sex rises from the warm, damp place where she sat. She lowers Harman's head onto the pillow without disturbing the grits, steps into her red heels, and eases toward the window. She hears sounds like a corroded metal door.

Her fingers touch the switch to the floodlights. Then she stops. Instead, she flicks off the kitchen lights. Her pupils spiral open.

Charlene grips the long handle of the thin blinds, slowly turns it. Slanted rays of moonlight slice across her face, neck, and bare shoulders. In the darkness beside the garage, the headlights of wrecked cars flicker like fireflies when the clouds unveil the moonlight. Nothing moves. She trains her eyes on the open garage, then trails back toward the wrecks, raking the darkness.

A spark of light reflects in the headlights of one of the cars. Charlene mistakes the flicker for movement. Her eyes stare into the bulbous night eyes of the wrecked car. Only when she hears the soft, distant hum of an engine does she realize the glint as a reflection from a passing car. Still her wide pupils are fixed on the wreck's headlights, its eyes reflecting now in hers. She recalls with instant clarity what she witnessed inside that hollow car, and savors her hot nakedness against the thin dress.

She had seen the mystery that could hide out there, inside the shell that held those eyes. Walking back in a daydream after checking the sunflowers behind Harman's garage, Charlene had caught sight of movement inside one of the wrecks. She'd stopped. She'd waited. Something stirred inside her. There were no sounds; everything was still.

She moved quietly, and after entering the rear door of the garage, Charlene slipped off her shoes. She stopped and listened. Her pulse throbbed in her neck. Slowly and carefully, she opened the aluminum ladder that rested against the side wall and climbed without sound to the top step, where she could see through the opening at the eaves, down into the car just beyond the wall. She didn't know the boy's name. He was one of the neighborhood boys, maybe fourteen. He was shirtless, his dungarees wilted at his ankles. She saw nearly the full length of him. His head lay back, his thin neck taunt as muscle, eyes closed. Sweat coiled down his face. His brown chest and stomach were covered with sweat. She was no more than fifteen feet from him. He was in full view. She watched everything until he finished. This was July fourth.

Charlene sits on the floor inches from her sofa, at eye level with the tower of white grits in Harman's ear, and pulls off her red heels. She presses forward and whispers, "Whore heels, r-e-d whore heels."

Outside, she moves stealthily through the moonlight to the corner of the small house, looks and listens, eyes wide, ears filled with the thin pitch of acute silence. There is movement inside the garage, somewhere in the shadows. The grass is wet and cool on her bare feet. She kneels beside the Mustang. Suddenly, its metal snaps, contracting in the cool night, sending a surge of fear up the backs of her legs, into her buttocks. Charlene is outside herself now, within and without at once. Silent. Motionless. She feels a second wave of cool night air, feels the thin dress against her nipples.

In darkness, she follows the line of nandinas to the giant fig trees at the corner of the garage. She stands and waits; moon shadows stamp her cheek the shape of a fig leaf. Charlene passes imperceptibly, furtively, from the shadows to the corner of the garage. She turns, looks behind her, into the darkness. Charlene closes her eyes and listens. Nothing. She reaches for the light just inside the garage, feels along the hot metal wall for the switch, finds it. The fluorescent lights flutter and whine.

A fat, black possum freezes, hovering over the cat's dish. Its black, surly eyes are wide and dripping wet. Charlene moves slowly through the heavy odor of sawdust, grease, and gasoline toward it. The eyes of the possum follow her as Charlene lifts a spider-webbed two iron from a dusty black golf bag near the die press.

For a third time, she feels the sensation of being an observer of her own actions. She steps toward the possum. It shrinks in retreat under a wooden tool bench. Charlene raises the two iron, then stops and smiles broadly as the cartoon image of the possum's small head arching like a divot above the garage floor takes shape in her mind.

The possum inches backward, withdrawing into the shadows beneath the cluttered worktable, wedging itself against a bucket of thick, black motor oil. She can see his eyes behind the paint cans and bucket. Charlene prods with the iron. She feels the possum's body give. She lays the two iron on the table and takes a cigarette from a pack Harman left there. She smokes. The possum means nothing to her.

She takes another cigarette, lights it from the first. The possum means nothing to her.

Charlene crosses the garage, glancing back at her kitchen window. To anyone standing there, she would appear to be on stage, here in the florescent garage lights. She turns ever so slowly, eyes half shut, and saunters across the cement floor, smoking, thinking of all those eyes out there, those eyes bathing her. I'll show him, she thinks.

She switches off the lights, pulls hard on her cigarette, waits for her eyes to adjust to the darkness. Behind Charlene, she hears paint cans scrape the cement, reaches again for the light switch. The possum is caught in the open. It freezes.

"Play dead," she whispers.

She backs slowly away from it, pulling the chain that lowers the garage door, never taking her eyes from him. She glances around the garage, finds a galvanized foot tub and a cement block. She takes the handle of the tub, drags it across the cement behind her toward the possum, which cowers in a corner.

"Sounds like a tornado, don't it?" she says. .

Back inside her house, Charlene disconnects the hose from the vacuum cleaner, fishes around in the back of the unit for an attachment. She finds her old electric hair clippers and a half roll of duct tape above the washing machine. The keys to the Mustang are in the orange Clemson ashtray. Charlene can't resist touching the volcano of crusty cold grits rising from Harman's ear. "That is something to build on," she whispers.

She shifts into reverse and backs the Mustang into the garage, duct tapes the vacuum hose to the car's chrome exhaust pipe, and presses the head of the hose into the knife-shaped attachment. After sliding the cement block to the edge of the foot tub under which the possum is trapped, Charlene lifts its handle and inches the vacuum attachment underneath, slides the block back into place, and seals the tub all around with duct tape.

She fires up the Mustang, pumping the exhaust under the foot tub, waits and thinks:

"Something is wrong," Charlene whispers. She wants it to be in her head. She felt it start in her heart, then lodge in her head. She wants it to be something that can be surgically removed. She wants the thing to go away.

She rests her elbows on the hood, pulls hard on the cigarette, presses her body against the Mustang's warm headlight, feels the engine's heat begin to accumulate in her belly.

Months earlier she had hoped it was not in her head, that instead her body was concealing something from her, something she shouldn't know about. After Doctor Vick examined her, he said she was as fit as a fiddle.

She reached into her bag and handed him a soft plastic eye she'd bought at South Of The Border. "You can have it," she said.

"This would look good in a fish bowl," he said. He sneezed four times in quick succession and said to her, "You're as fit as a fiddle."

"No I'm not," Charlene said. "Look again."

This time Vick said her tonsils were maybe a little larger than normal.

"I was thinking more along the lines of a tumor," she'd said.

Charlene didn't tell the doctor what was at stake. She was looking for something to fix things.

When Charlene told Harman she was going to have her tonsils out, he gave her a devilish smile and said, "This could make a world of difference."

The possum is almost dead from the Mustang's exhaust, but not quite. After she lays it on its thick belly atop the barbecue grill, Charlene can see its lungs slowly rise and fall. Still she's taking no chances. She pulls a length of duct tape, rips it off the roll, then tears long quarter-inch strips. She pulls the legs outward and securely tapes the possum spread-eagle to the bars of the grill, then tapes its snout. The possum does not resist.

Charlene plugs one end of the heavy orange extension cord into the wall socket, then plugs the clipping shears into the other end. She turns on the old paint-spattered radio and finds a late night oldies station, turns the volume up so she can hear the music over the humming of the clippers. Starting at the hindquarters, she slowly glides the clippers up one side of the fat possum. She works slowly and purposefully. The hair falls into the grill basin. She sings along with the Righteous Brothers and Percy Sledge. From time to time she touches the head of the clippers to her cheek, making sure they are not too hot. When she has clipped as closely as possible, Charlene stands back and looks at her work.

A two-inch wide Mohawk runs down the possum's spine.

Charlene reaches into a tool cabinet for a wire brush. On a shelf near the radio, she finds a spray can of upholstery glue.

"Are we playing dead?" she says in a voice that frightens her a little.

The possum shows the first signs of life when Charlene runs the steel brush up the Mohawk, forcing the hair to stand up on its back. She sprays glue as she goes. The hair stands up like quills on the possum's back. She must wait for the glue to dry.

Charlene opens the door to her kitchen. She looks over at the sofa and imagines the combined effect of the grits in the ear and Harman's head, Mohawked. She returns to the garage carrying a steaming aluminum pot, a dish towel, and Harman's razor. The soft voice of Art Garfunkle singing "I Only Have Eyes For You" drifts over the night air. The possum vibrates when Charlene lays the smoking wet rag on the animal's side, its eyes wild and richly black. She applies the shaving cream in small patches and shaves the areas she trimmed while the glue dries on the Mohawk.

When she is nearly finished, Paul McCartney begins "Yesterday" and she cries. She lays Harman's razor on the grill and sits on the foot tub. Charlene bends forward, rocking back and forth, her palms wet with tears. When the sobbing stops, she goes to the Mustang for her cigarettes, returns to the foot tub, sits and smokes. She wipes the last of the tears and sweat on the hem of her black and white polka-dotted dress, exposing her sex to the possum, who stares between her legs.

Charlene completes the shaving, washes the razor, and drops it in the trashcan. It rattles down between discarded oil filters, out of sight. She returns to the grill with a spray can of red automobile paint. She squats eye level beside the possum, then slowly and carefully sprays the Mohawk. She steps back, studies her work. She circles the possum, then starts back to the Mustang. She sits in the driver's seat and smokes. She catches sight of her face in the mirror, reaches for lipstick–red, the color of her heels. She applies the red glaze, then applies it again, so thick that her lips look like Halloween wax. She takes a deep breath and a bead of sweat races down between her breasts. Charlene unsnaps the top two buttons of her dress. She tilts the mirror, grips the wheel, looks up at herself in the mirror again and smiles.

She walks a slow circle around the possum. She can feel its eyes follow her, although they don't appear to move. She stops at the possum's head, leans forward. The Mohawk is firm and deeply red. Charlene presses her index finger to her lips, scooping red lipstick. She slowly presses the marsupial's neck with her left hand, inching forward, increasing the pressure as she goes. Percy Faith is on the radio. "I could cut off your head, too," she says. She lays her hand over its head. The possum's skull fits into the palm like a tiny breast. She applies her full weight. The grill slowly gives. Charlene covers the possum's mouth with red lipstick.

Charlene opens the glove box of the Mustang for tissues. She wipes the lipstick from her fingers, and, returning the tissues, finds Harman's toenail clippers. After lifting the grill top and placing it gently on the cement floor, Charlene clips the duct tape that secures the possum. Leaving the lights burning in the garage, she crosses the cool, wet grass to her backdoor. She doesn't turn and look.

Inside the kitchen, she reaches for a small, yellow pot her mother used for boiling hypodermic needles. Charlene adds water from the spigot. The gas burner makes a huffing sound at the moment of combustion, its flame more yellow than blue. She turns the control knob, forming a small red and violent crown of fire. She centers the small pot on the burner. Sweat rolls down into one of her ears. Her dress sticks to her damp thighs like thin, crushed paper as she reaches up to the cabinet for the box of grits. She pours a measured amount into the boiling water, cuts the burner down to a blue halo.

Charlene showers and dries with a beach towel. The words *Cherry Grove, South Carolina*, are printed in faded red letters across it. She stands naked, looking into the drawer where Harman kept his work shirts, finds one of his Atlanta Braves tee shirts, so worn she can see through it when she holds it up to the light. She pulls the shirt over her head and walks barefoot back to the living room. She goes to the window with the air conditioner—the window that gives her the best view into the garage—and lifts the blinds. She can see him there in the soft light, see the red fin rising from gray skin the color of flesh turned inside out. He has moved away from the grill, but not outside the garage. He is still drunk from the exhaust. She watches his awkward waltz. She waits. Without taking her eyes from her creation, Charlene feels for the controls of the air conditioner, turns the blower up a notch, then leans forward. She looks down at her breasts, inches now from the air conditioner vents. Her nipples harden, ache, then burn. She looks up again, out toward the garage.

Behind her, atop the blue eye of the stove, the thin pot begins its violent vibrations. Charlene's nipples are on fire. She stares without expression through the freshly polished glass window, out across the yard at the primitive animal, its thin, loose skin a waterlogged gray, its Mohawk firm and fiercely red. Its steps are tentative, like a baby's first steps. Then it freezes, turns and looks back at her as if to speak. Charlene smiles, which suddenly brings her reflection into view; Harman's vacant eyes stare from above the pillow on the sofa behind her.

"I dare you," she hisses. "I just dare you."

What The Arraignment Meant
Gary and Sheila Powers

You can take it or leave it. I'm not saying I'm blameless. I'm not saying that none of the charges are true, that none of this is my fault. What I'm asking for is an open mind, that's all. I'm saying there is a starting point to every event, and where people place that starting point can make one heck of a difference.

What I'm saying is that when I held my mother's face in my stubby little five-year-old hands and kissed her, her eyes got all watery and she said, "You weren't supposed to be born," like I was the most precious thing on earth. That's one place to start. And later, when I was thirteen and secretly taped her calls and threatened to play them back for my Dad, she said the same thing, only a lot louder. "You should'a never been born," she screamed. Then she huffed out of the room. That's a second point of departure. After their divorce I told Mom I never should have been born. She added ice to her vodka and said, "It's not your fault." She understood, she said. That's launching pad number three.

You want the truth, and I'm trying my best to tell it. But a paid-for-ticket at the wrong gate gets you nowhere, wouldn't you say? So where is the starting point, I mean where do you begin?

I for one would like to start by saying I don't like the prosecutor doing what he's doing when he refers to me by name. Gary Powers, that's my name. That's a fact. But he's trying to turn coincidence into something it's not, or maybe he's appealing to something deep and mean in people, trying to squeeze out every ounce of meanness in their brain. It's hard for people to do good, hard enough without somebody bringing the devil out in them. So what if my first name is Francis? Nobody, I mean nobody, ever, ever called me Francis, not once, never. I can't help it if a guy who was never supposed to be born arrived on earth the day the Russians shot down the U2.

When my mother recovered from the anesthesia, she said, "It is a sign. A baby is born who was never supposed to be here. And on the same day a man is shot down who was never supposed to be there. For every Ying there must be a Yang."

Everybody thought the pilot was dead or was going to be shortly. "And both this man and my baby have the same last name. There is a meaning there."

My mother named me and my Dad, no bookworm, signed the papers. He came to hate me. Francis. No son of mine, he'd say. From the day I was born until the day he blew himself to smithereens fooling with the gas grill in the backyard, he never forgave my mother for naming me Francis, and never forgave me for wearing it either.

The point is the prosecutor keeps referring to me always as Francis Gary Powers, I mean every time. Now you tell me, what do people think? Traitor? A man who ought to kill himself but doesn't have the nerve? Or assassin? You bet. Lee Harvey Oswald. John Wilkes Booth. James Earl Ray. Mark David Chapman. Now do you think these guys went through their lives with three names? No way. Only after they killed somebody did they get the three. I don't like it. Prosecutors did it to them. What is the effect on the jury? If you can get them thinking in triplicate, if you get their juices moving in that direction, if you get their brain tuned in to channel C.O.P.S., that's a finger on the switch. I mean I keep getting the feeling that I'm an X on a mall map, and no matter where I go the little light above my head says You Are Here. To tell you the truth, it is the feeling that things are happening, things outside my control. You hear your name spelled out like that and it gets to you, makes you feel that you are outside events, like you've become a label for something else, something bad.

I'll say it again. I'm not saying I'm blameless. I'm saying let the facts speak for themselves. I'm saying let's have a clear picture. I mean, say these words out loud: Little. Debbie's. Cakes. Say those words over and over. Go ahead. Say it three times.

Voice of a child molester.

Think about it long enough and it can mean anything. There's more than one side. I just want to make that clear. You've got your Yang. I just want to have my say.

First off, I never complained about the rent and I loved my wife. But when you pay your rent and you don't complain, and you love your wife, you expect certain things in return. Especially when you do little things like a coat of paint here and a replaced window there and you don't present a bill to your landlord. I even fixed the furnace once. Would have cost Crupper fifty bucks, minimum. And I was never more than five days late on the rent. Never. You expect Crupper to hold up his end. That's what I'm saying. You have certain expectations. And you don't want him sleeping with your wife. No matter how low the rent is. No matter. You want to know, so I'll tell you.

August in Darlington, South Carolina. No air conditioning. Something dead under the house.

It was the smell. Could have been a cat or a possum, a coon or a dog. Could have been something else. Whatever it was was definitely dead. And it was under the kitchen. The air conditioner had been out for two days. Went out in the middle of the night. Sheila and I, Sheila, that's my wife if you haven't figured it out already. Just for the record, Sheila and I were sleeping on the kitchen floor. We put the fan on the kids and then found the coolest place to put down our mattress. It's a thick cement floor with green and white Formica squares on top. The smell still came through.

I said to Sheila, "I won't call Crupper until the morning. No reason to wake him. Nothing he can do in the middle of the night." That's the kind of man I am. Just for the record.

Sheila said, "It wouldn't kill him to know, the heartless jerk." Her breath smelled of vodka and menthol. "I say wake up Mr. Unreliable."

But I didn't. I'm not that kind of guy.

I didn't know then what I know now.

I left messages on Crupper's machine the first day. I left more messages the next morning. That afternoon, The Darlington County Bank sign said 101 degrees as I drove home from work. The woman on the car radio gave the heat index every ten minutes. 119 she said, describing the heat the way some people describe sex dreams. When I pulled into our treeless yard, mirage waves hovered around our small, brick house, distorting the lines of the walls and the black roof.

Sheila said first thing when I walked in, "We're eating out." The fan blew full blast, sending the dead rot ricocheting off the walls.

"It don't smell so bad," I lied. "I think it may be going away." She just looked at me. She'd been at home all day, in the house, in her bra and underwear, watching the cool anchorwoman warn that it was too hot to let the kids play outside. She'd plotted the rising heat index with a black marker on the kitchen wall, gripped the fly swatter all day to tame the kids.

We only have one car.

I drove us to one of those all-you-can-eat salad bars. They have to keep it cool there. When I was parking the car, I thought I'd try to liven things up a little, change the mood. "This is the fat farm," I said to Toby. Toby's my five-year-old. "This is where people come to pig out." While we were standing in line, Sheila kept smelling the children's clothes and pulling them close to her, away from the other customers. "We'll be here forever," she snarled. "What's time to a pig?" said little Toby.

Lying on the kitchen floor that night, Sheila said, "If I was a man, I'd be kicking me some butt about now."

"What am I supposed to do? You call, you leave a message. The guy won't return your calls."

We laid there watching the ever-shifting pattern of fruit flies in the moonlight. Neither of us said anything for a while. The smell really came through at night.

"I'd say it's time to take action," she said. I didn't say anything. "Goodnight, Francis," she said.

The next day I went to Crupper's office. He wasn't really a real estate man, you know. He just rented a couple of houses that belong to his wife. He's a heating and air conditioning guy. Doesn't even have a secretary. When I knocked on the door, I guess he could tell from the knock that I meant business. His office windows were covered with that black smoky plastic stuff that dope dealers put on their car windows. So I say to myself, this guy won't even answer the door. At that point I'm thinking, what's he so afraid of? So I turn the knob, and sure enough the joint is open.

A door closes at the back of the small building. I walk to his office where it's cool. The place is a pigpen. Papers everywhere, you name it. I hear a truck start up outside. I open the back door, and guess who is racing away? Now Sheila begins to make sense to me. He's a weasel, a coward. So I say, he's got to come back sooner or later. We'll talk rent and deposits, we'll talk rental agreements and legal action, we'll talk dead things and cool air. He's got to come back sooner or later, I say to myself.

I pick up the phone to call my boss, Ransom Fields. I figure I'll tell him my car broke down and I'm near heat stroke, that I won't be back in today. What's Fields gonna say, I say to myself.

But I don't.

I press the redial button on Crupper's phone. I don't know why, the result of some chemical connection in my brain maybe. It rings twice.

Sheila answers.

"Hello? *Sheila*? That you?"

"Don't tell me you decided against going to Crupper's office, huh? What's your excuse? Don't tell me the car broke down again

Do you know that it's ten days before the rent is due? We got no leverage for ten days. Any man who really loved his wife–"

"You are absolutely right," I said. "I'll take care of it. I'm not leaving this office until he comes back here. It'd take a SWAT team to get me out of here before he gets back. You've got my word on that. If it takes all day and all night–"

"It's not bad enough," she was screaming into the phone now, "that a landlord won't get a dead animal from under a woman's kitchen, it's not bad enough that he lies, and lies, and lies about . . . everything–"

"Lies about what," I say. "What do you mean? Since when did you talk to Crupper?"

'"It's been weeks," Sheila stammered.

My brain does a sudden 180.

"Just you see to it that we don't die of heat," she said. "Or of this smell." She was shouting again.

I wasn't afraid of what she might say next. Only I knew that at the end of it she would say goodbye, Francis. So I hung up. I pressed the redial button on his phone again. It didn't even ring before she picked up. All I heard was a big in-suck of air. Then I hung up again.

I buried the thermostat needle. I waited. I waited all night. By morning, I could see my breath. Crupper never came back. Left the place open, the lights on, the condensation rolling down the inside of the black plate glass window like big, fat elephant tears.

I didn't even phone in work the next morning. I'd been up all night. Had time to read the scribble on the desk calendar, look through his desk, find an envelope full of Motel 6 receipts, peruse the stack of cards and letters in the bottom drawer, do a little two-plus-two arithmetic, press the redial button a few times.

The next morning around ten when I got home, the house was cool. There was a bill on the kitchen table.

The whole place smelled like perfume. Sheila was still in her housecoat. She didn't look like she'd slept much, but her face had that real pink blushed look like someone who exercises regularly. Which means she looked different. She didn't even ask me where I'd been all night. She said first thing, "The kids spent the night at the sitter's. I couldn't put them through another night of that heat. I was here all alone. It's gone. It was a dead possum under the house. I've got to do some laundry."

In a sort of daze, I staggered over to the thermostat and turned it down to forty, which is as low as it goes. I put my hand over the vent.

Sheila walked past me with a roll of damp sheets off our bed. "Everything's fine now," she said. Meaning the air.

The heat wave continued. A few days later, she said, "I don't believe it, but I think something *else* is dead under the house. I don't believe it."

"Believe it," I said. "You've got your air conditioning. You can put up with the smell."

You should have seen the look on Crupper's face.

You want to know why, so I'll tell you. I've had some time to think about it. I'm not trying to be philosophical. I'm not one of those guys who knocks on your door and hands out religious materials. I'm just a guy who loves his wife, who wants to come home to a cool house in the summer, who wants to be appreciated and understood, who wants to, you know, do the right thing. It just so happens I'm a guy who pays his rent on time. It just so happens there was something dead under the house. It just so happens I'm a guy with three names.

Murmurs
John W. Stuckey

My heart keeps me awake at night. I lie there wishing it would stop, praying that it doesn't. The hours go by. I've lost the sounds of night to my heart. And I miss them. There was a time when sleep was meaningless to me, when a locomotive five blocks away meant no more to my ears than a feather swooning down from a limber pine. There was a time when I didn't even know I had a heart, when I wasn't aware of its beating, I mean. There was a time when being reminded that I was alive was a happy thing.

Now I just lie there with my faulty heart with its faulty valve, both of which are, I want to believe, the fault of the manufacturers. Sometimes deep into the night, listening instead of sleeping, I hear it speak to me in its little mechanical voice, nagging, reminding me that we are forever linked. Saying to me we have no life apart. Like Siamese twins we hold a mutual hatred for trespassers. We dumpster-dive for the magic word that will free one of us, leave the other to fend for himself. We listen for that word with our one good ear.

I know how it feels to be in a bad marriage although I've never been married, never expect to be.

Eventually, I fall into exhausted half sleep, which usually begins with the soft light of dawn and lasts until the sun seeps over the earth's edge and pries open my eyes. For these sweet moments my heart becomes a music box, tinkling its lullaby over the blood that rushes with the sweet sound of cellos through its chambers. And I sleep. Sometimes I even dream.

God keeps teaching me a thing or two about hearts. About what happens when they are opened and closed, about human tinkering. The lessons have been coming for a long time.

Somehow I knew even at age twelve that it would come to something like this. My father died of a heart attack that summer. I don't remember thinking too much about it at the time. He was thirty-five, the age I am now. It about killed my mother, though. For years afterward she slept maybe fifteen hours a day.

The point is, I was left with a lot of time on my hands. Out of nervous energy, I suppose, I did little pranks. Stuff kids do. I wish now that I hadn't. It was nothing really malicious, understand. I mean I never hurt anybody. Just kid stuff. Some of it was pretty funny, at the time. I've made it a point to keep up my sense of humor. It's gotten me this far.

One Sunday when I was thirteen, the preacher announced that the Methodist Youth Fellowship was selling bumper stickers to raise money for the American Cancer Society or the Heart Fund or something. So everybody bought one. The sticker said, "Christ is Lord." The next Sunday during the service, Evander Baker and I waited in the parking lot. We had permanent Magic Markers. Black ones. We changed all the O's to A's, turning the Lord into lard. As we worked, we shouted out things we liked cooked in grease. "Fried chicken," he'd yell. "Pork chops," I'd call back. We laughed until we about croaked.

During the thundering chorus of "Just A Closer Walk With Thee," I shouted, "Hey Evander, praise the lard!" He came out from between two cars, rocking stiff-backed and laughing like a lunatic, squeezing his penis so hard it must have been the color of a radish. He could hardly catch his breath. "Stop it, man," he gasped in a squeaky voice. "I'm gonna wet my pants."

Before the service was over, we walked the short distance to Baker's Grocery, which his uncle owned, and bought a Pepsi from the outside machine. We sat on a bench out front and read the bumper stickers, smiled, and waved to folks as they passed on their way home.

Later, Evander told. Same day.

More than one person said that God would remember. I believe them now. Evander apologized before the congregation the next Sunday. I just never went back. People gave me dirty looks, and when they did I'd stare back or I'd suddenly burst into tears, pretending of course the whole time, until they felt like crap and said they were sorry. "I'm just a kid," I'd sob. And if it was a woman who'd given me the dirty look and if she had some boobs, I'd let her press my face into them. I'd cry until she did. Sometimes I'd hold my breath and just feel my face against their warm softness. I'd hear her heart beating.

Now, the only heart I hear is my own. And what it sounds like, in the words of my former attorney, Mr. Mcfarland, is "loose change dancing a jig." No amount of crying will get me that close to a woman's breast again.

I don't feel sorry for myself. My job prevents that. But I'm just annoyed a lot of the time. I want some peace and quiet. It's not as if I'm without friends. The folks at the office are a great bunch. They're like my family. They are all I've got.

I'm still pretty much a jokester, and I can take it as well as give it out. So when I arrive late for work, as I usually do, all baggy-eyed and sloshing coffee everywhere, Lisa will say, "Slow down, Stuckey, you're sounding like a tornado siren this morning. We all about went down under our desk when you got off the elevator." And I'll say, "Shoot, Lisa, since when did you need a reason to go down?" And my day will begin. I don't know what I'd do without them sometimes.

We all have our computers and our crazy clients. Some of us are Food Stamps. I'm AFDC. You have to work at not getting too cynical, at not being too judgmental. We all like to laugh, when we can. So we tell sex jokes. The women in the office always know the most sex jokes. Some of them are real dirty. Some are filthy. Before I went to work at Social Services eight years ago, I never would have guessed.

We had a meeting two months ago and Lana, that's our supervisor, read us the State's definition of sexual harassment, which covered almost everything we do at the office. Afterwards, we all agreed that if any one of us ever said or did anything that hurt somebody's feelings, we'd say so. We all promised we would. As we were leaving the meeting, I put my hand on Shonda's back, giving it a soft rub and said, "Looks like the fun's over." She glanced back at my hand and said, "I'll give you exactly two hours to stop that."

Everybody at the office said I should see a lawyer, and so finally, after three years, I did. I thought to myself, maybe I really do get on their nerves. Mcfarland was the attorney's name. He about crapped with joy when I told him why I'd come. "Jeraldine! Jeraldine, goddammit," he shouted. Jeraldine was his secretary in the next room. "Jeraldine!! Shut off that goddamn mu-zak."

When the room was quiet, he stood up and leaned his ear toward me, near my chest, squinting his eyes, and then whispered, "Good God 'omighty." He dove into his desk drawer. "Damn it to hell," he muttered. "Where the hell is that tape measure?"

He found it and handed me the hook at the head of the tape. "Back up slow," he said. I began slowly stepping back. "How long ago did you say?" he asked.

"Three years ago."

"And it's been like this ever since?"

"From the time they..."

"Shhh," he said, holding his finger to his lips, tilting his head up, eyes closed like a blind man. "Back," he whispered, "back." I was already out the door in the middle of the hall. "Stop!" he shouted. He looked down at the tape. "Thirty feet. Thirty goddamn feet. The sonofabitch is audible at thirty feet." He snapped the tape from my fingers and began reeling it in. "At twenty-five thousand a foot, I figure...." He broke concentration for a second. "What kind of work do you do?"

"Desk job," I said. He looked disappointed. He thought for a second.

"Who do you work for?"

"The State," I said. "Social Services."

"Damned government," he said.

Mcfarland pressed a button on the side of the large silver tape measure and the remaining few feet zipped inside.

"Boy," he said, "after today you can *buy* fucking Social Services."

When I told them at work, everybody started saying I'd be cleaning out my desk soon. There were all kinds of sex jokes about wealthy men and smart women. And somebody started a wish list on the wall in the lounge, and everybody wrote their name on a separate sheet of paper and started their own list. At first there were new cars and vacations to Disney World and new carpet. Then people started putting things on other people's lists, like sex lube jell and vibrators and stuff. Lana, the supervisor, said that stuff had to come down, that it wouldn't be understood by folks in Columbia or Washington, that it had to come down from public view. So she taped it up in her office, and people drifted in at break time and read the new additions or added their own. There was always laughter coming from Lana's office.

One day, Jimmy, who was working as receptionist, buzzed me. "I think the FBI is here," he whispered. When I walked up front, I was met by a tall professionally handsome man in his late forties.

"Richardson's the name," he said. "I represent Baxley International." I guess I was still giving him the FBI fish-eye once-over. "Baxley Healthcare," he continued. "I was hoping you would be free for lunch," he said, lifting his briefcase. Jimmy was humming "Money-Money-Money-Monnn-ey"" when Mr. Richardson and I walked out. I glanced back and saw Shonda leaning over Jimmy looking at Richardson. "He looks like he ought to be in the stories," she said.

For an hour and a half we ate our steaks, or rather I did. "Just call me Richard," he insisted, buying the first of my five bourbons. All the doctors said I shouldn't drink. But what the hell. What the hell.

"Richard Richardson??" I said after the third drink.

"You can call me Rich if you'd like," he said. While I ate and drank he showed me charts and computer readouts and four-color brochures. You'd be surprised by the things that a heart can take. I was, anyway. He talked a lot about saving lives and what quality of life really meant. Finally after I'd finished my fourth bourbon, I looked at him as straight in the eye as I could and said, "What do you want?"

"Nothing," he said. "Just a chance to be heard. Just wanted to leave you with a few things to think about."

"That's all?" I slurred.

"That's it."

"Hell, I'm never short on things to think about," I said.

"I hope you'll communicate your feelings about all this to your attorney–" he looked at his pad, "Mr. McFarland."

"Let me buy you a drink," I said. He'd ordered one before the meal but he hadn't touched it.

When we got back to the office, he wanted to shake hands in the Lexus. "Hell no," I said. "I want you to meet some people."

Nobody was at the desk up front when Richie and I walked in. But I remembered the code to the inside door; they have to keep it locked, you know. Some of our clients come in drunk or stoned. You have hell getting them out once they get in.

I burped real loud on the elevator going up. I just cracked up.

As I passed the first couple of offices I realized they were empty, the lights out. "Yooo-hooo," I said. Richie wanted to stop right there, retreat back to the Lexus, but I had a pretty good hold on his Brooks Brothers. I dragged him into the office I share with Lisa, Steve, Synthea, and Brenda. I reached for the light.

The girls from the office had formed two lines in front of the desks, each one of them wearing a little grass skirt they'd made from shredded paper. Carmichael, who was near the door, pressed the button on his ghetto box and "Heartbreak Hotel" blasted across the room. The women all shimmied in their skirts, and I hunched up the line with my thumbs inside my belt, singing like a dead Elvis, only louder. Steve moved up the line beside me, my bodyguard. And Lana, our boss, stood waiting at my desk with a crown somebody had made from cardboard and silver wrapping paper.

The girls did little fake fainting spells as I hunka, hunka, hunka burnin' love past them. Rachel, who weighs about 270, took my face between her cream puff hands and kissed me right on the mouth. Then she stumbled back like it had done something for her.

When the song was over, Lana put the crown on my head and proclaimed me King of Hearts. Mr. Richardson stood leaning against the door in the back, smiling. I don't think anybody had noticed him. I couldn't for the life of me remember his name. When I did remember it, he was gone.

I was the last one to leave the office that afternoon. I always like to clean up my desk. A clean start each day does me a world of good. So I was alone on the elevator. I could hear my faulty heart all the way down. By the time the bell chimed and the double doors slowly opened, I felt like crying. I turned up the radio loud when I got in the car to drive home.

A few weeks later, Lana called me into her office. She said that she was having some surgery and would be out of work for at least three weeks. "It could be longer," she said. "Could be six weeks." Everybody knew she was going in for a boob job. You could tell that when she was young she'd been a knockout. "I need to know," she said, "if I should ask for a replacement for you."

"Why does everybody seem to think I want to quit?" I said.

"Because you won't have to work when you get your settlement," she said. "Maybe you think you would, but you won't. Why should you?"

"This is all lawyer talk. That's all. I'll believe it when I can write checks on it."

"When they send a three-piece suit to take you out to lunch, that means something," she said. "I don't have to know today, but if you know when you might be leaving it'd make it easier on everybody."

When I got back to my office, there was a message to call Mcfarland.

I held the phone about a foot from my ear. It was the goddamned government this, and the goddamned government that, and there's no way to get the bastards, and there's no justice for the common man.

When he was done shouting, the best I could figure was this: If a manufacturer of heart valves makes a valve that is approved by the Food and Drug Administration, the manufacturer can't be sued. Period.

"But nobody told me I'd be a walking tambourine for the rest of my life," I said.

"Those goddamned bastards," he began again. Finally he said he thought he had a good chance of winning the case if he could fight it far enough, but there was no way he could do it on spec. I'd have to pay. I'd get it back ten thousand times over when we won. But I'd have to pay.

When Lana came back from her surgery, we all threw a surprise party for her, with gifts and party hats. You could look at her chest and tell they'd done some work there, some fine work. There were a thousand boob jokes. And all the guys begged her to let us see them. She assured us that they were in no condition to be seen at the time, but that she wasn't closing off all possibilities for the future. The girls in the office bought her a bathing suit and insisted she open the box to give us a hint of what to expect. We guys had bought her a gift too, but we made her promise that she would join the party when it moved to The Paradise Lounge. The Paradise Lounge is a bar where those of us who have nobody to go home to go after work sometimes.

Lana called for a sitter–she's been divorced for four or five years–and at five o'clock we took the Japanese elevator down. The elevator became Japanese by squashing people in until the doors would barely close. Bells rang all the way down.

As it turned out, it was Karaoke Night at The Paradise Lounge, and people were singing. Lisa and Brenda and Shonda did "Leader of the Pack" and "My Boyfriend's Back." Jimmy, the guy who trouble-shoots electrical problems in our building, sang "Midnight Hour." A lot of other people sang too. The place was really crowded. Maybe I was just at that point when the liquor for a split second settles everything, lines it up so that all things point in the same direction. I don't know what I'm trying to say. But I looked up at everybody, and everybody was so happy, everybody.

The DJ, or whatever you call the Karaoke guy, took a break, and Russ handed over Lana's gift. She opened the box and held up its contents, a flaming red knit sweater. It must have been at least three sizes too small.

"You boys ain't got one brain between you," Shonda said, holding the sweater up in front of Lana. "There ain't enough thread here to cover *one* of these boobs." Everybody laughed.

"Show her, Jimmy, show her," yelled Russ over the noise.

Jimmy lifted the right sleeve of the sweater. On the inside was a tiny switch. With Lisa's help, they had sewn in hair-thin wires that attached to two little lights on the front of the sweater where Lana's nipples would be. Jimmy pushed the switch one way and one side blinked, pushed it the other and the other side blinked.

"Turn signals," I said. "We don't want any accidents on the job."

I'm no singer. Never have been. Probably one of those things I would have learned in church, had I gone. But a band of fools requires foolishness in equal parts from each. I looked down the list of hundreds of songs to find something that wouldn't hurt the audience. My name was called.

"In the town, where I was born," I began. The song was "Yellow Submarine," and to my delight everybody, I mean everybody, sang the chorus. People put their arms around one another and rocked from side to side and sang. They held up their drinks to one another or to me. "We all live in a yellow submarine," they sang, packed against one another, not wishing to be any other place. Then came the part in the middle of the song that I'd forgotten, a little brief part where there are a couple of spoken lines. I never understood those lines. Everybody stopped singing. I felt it was my responsibility to get them smiling again. Over the spoken lines of the song are sounds of the submarine's engine room.

I didn't even think about it. I put the microphone to my chest. The engine room filled the bar. The place went bananas. You should have seen their faces. Their eyes flew open like spring loaded shades and their mouths fell open, and then they laughed in a rising wave that swept over me. Except for one person.

She was standing near the speaker, blondish brown hair, thin, squinting a little as if she'd left her glasses at home. The thing is, her expression didn't change when my heart played its solo. It was going cha-ching, cha-ching, pretty much in time with the song, and my friends from the office were going down on the floor; Jimmy was banging his face on the table. But the girl with the wrinkly eyes up front didn't change her expression at all. The same as when someone tells a joke and the other person just doesn't get the punch line.

By the time I got back to our table, there were two drinks waiting for me already. Somebody had put Lana's name on the list to sing a Dolly Parton song, and then there were more drinks. But I found myself looking at the girl near the speaker. I say girl, but she was not much younger than me. She stood in the same place, near the little stage, clearly in a world of her own—not unhappy, mind you—as happy as anyone there. But she seemed, the longer I looked at her, to be in her own little *Star Trek* beam-me-up column of light.

When I looked around again, all eyes were turned on Lana.

Every eye in the bar. She was walking back from the ladies' room in the red sweater that looked like paint on her skin. People smiled and opened a path for her. And when she wanted to make a turn, she'd stop, hit the blinker switch, and then make a right or a left. All the guys hooted, but nobody was ugly. When she got back to our tables, she gave each one of us a little hug and kissed us guys on the cheek. Her eyes were all watery and bright.

Now I wanted to sing. Wanted to. I couldn't get up there fast enough. I'd found my song. When the DJ called my name, I bounded forward. My friends and the people who'd heard me do "Yellow Submarine" all clapped.

I looked down at the girl near the speaker. She hadn't moved from her place. She looked at me and smiled. The music began.

I took a deep breath and sang. "I've got spurs that jingle, jangle, jingle . . . ." Everybody was singing again. After the second chorus, when there was just music, I put the microphone to my chest, raised one foot, then the other, and shook my imaginary spurs. The whole room wailed.

Joyous bodies convulsed in a community of hilarious ecstasy, bodies doubled over, breathless hands rising up in testimonial. The tears came down on the blushed, happy faces. Lisa and Brenda and Lana had their arms around one another, falling out in laughter, and by the end Jimmy and Steve were standing on their chairs, heads down, solemn, holding their flaming cigarette lighters up high.

I was laughing so hard I gave up on singing at all, held the microphone to my chest and jingle, jangle, jingled over the music.

But the girl just looked up, smiling, happy, but seeming to miss the performance. She seemed unaware of everybody else behind her.

I don't talk a very keen line. You can guess the reasons. After the operation, when I'd get really hard up, I'd go to noisy bars or discos and hit on the women who were anywhere near my league. But there would always come that point outside on the sidewalk, or in the car, when I'd get that funny look and the woman would say, "Do you hear that? What's that sound?" You should have seen the looks on their face when I told them. Some just sat there. Some, who were the social worker types, would ask if I wanted to talk about it. Some said stuff like, "You're shittin' me!" None of them were put in a very romantic mood. My confidence was eroded a little.

But there was the business of the girl standing up front. By the time Lisa, Shonda, Brenda, Lana and the others were paying up, I couldn't stop looking at her although she never once turned and looked back at me.

I'm the sort of guy who's the last to leave a party. I mean I don't stay around when it's clearly time for me to go, when I'm no longer wanted. But I figure that somebody has to be the last to leave. It's not like I have any pressing business. Usually I'll help clean up. I'm just not in a hurry to go home, that's all. So the gang all left, and suddenly the room seemed empty. I just sort of stood there, turning like a rotisserie in the middle of the floor. The DJ was sitting at a poker machine.

I walked up behind her. I thought she might just turn around on her own. I'm like that. I think that if you are in a room and you think hard enough about a person, she'll feel it somehow and turn and look at you. It almost never happens. When it does, though, it's magic.

So I was standing eight or ten feet behind her and it wasn't working. I took another step and then she turned. She smiled. "Oh, hi," she said. Her voice sounded like she was really drunk, snockered, I'd say. But her eyes weren't a bit drunk.

"Hi," I said. Then the cat got my tongue.

"I enjoyed your singing," she said, in that slurred voice again. Her eyes were wide and lively now, as if looking at me close-up she could finally see.

"Thanks," I said. "I noticed that you were about the only person who didn't sing." Her eyes followed my lips like they were sheet music or something. "You're not that shy, are you?"

She smiled and shook her head, and then I knew she was deaf.

Faith, that's her name, and I had a cup of coffee at the Waffle House on the Highway 52 by-pass. She said she was a computer programmer for the telephone company.

"Why did you go to The Paradise if you can't hear the music?" As soon as it started out of my mouth, I knew it was coming out wrong. But she didn't seem to mind.

"I like the people," she said. "I like to watch them have fun. I can feel the music when I stand near the speaker. And of course I can watch the people having fun. It really is contagious, isn't it?" she said. She didn't sound like a drunk to me now.

Before she left, I asked her if she thought she might have dinner with me some time, and she said she might.

I had one hell of a time getting to sleep. I'd almost doze off. Then I'd see Faith sitting across from me so close I could have taken her hand if I'd had the courage, and suddenly my heart would be rattling like a beggar's cup. I'd wake again. And I'd lie there. My mind would start up again.

If you've ever seen the scars, you know they're not a pretty sight. The body's not meant to be opened up. Nature provides the heart with all kinds of protection. There's no way not to leave scars.

Long ago I got into the habit of sleeping with a pillow on my chest. I tried ear plugs, but I was afraid the house would catch on fire. So I settle for a pillow. Holding that pillow there, I'm sure you can figure out what I think about sometimes. It helps just to have something in your arms.

So sometime near morning I went to sleep. And the damnedest thing happened. I was dreaming, but in my dream I was dreaming. It was the damnedest thing, really. I mean, in my dream I was watching myself dream. I was lying there and Faith was with me. I was sleeping quietly with her head on my chest, over my heart. And in my dream it was quiet. Everything was quiet except for our breathing. Our breathing was the only sound. Then she began to murmur in her sleep. At first I thought it was just her breathing, but it was a murmur, a voice, and then I understood what she was saying in her sleep, repeating the same words over and over.

"I can feel it," she said. "I can feel it."

Bird Blinding
Gale and Buzz Newcomb

Gale Newcomb lowered the receiver onto the cradle of the bedside telephone, then dragged her sewing chair to the closet, stepped up onto it, and felt along the high shelf for her husband's pistol. She gently patted the coarse, unfinished wood, working toward the end of the shelf. When her fingers met the revolver's thick, blunt chrome barrel, they rested there, then moved delicately down to the pistol's rough metal grip. For a moment, she allowed her index finger to trace the cold crescent trigger, then quickly pulled her hand away. She knew better than to take the gun down, to hide it or throw it into the field. She pushed the cool steel way back, thinking that maybe her husband would have one extra second to think about what that gun could do to a body.

She stepped down slowly and dragged the heavy chair back to the sewing table, placing the legs in the exact depressions they had formed in the bedroom carpet. She vacuumed over the chair's lines, erasing them. When she had tightly wound the cord and returned the vacuum to its assigned place in the closet, Gale walked quietly to the kitchen and dug inside her purse for lipstick. A pair of cardinals sputtered in the camellia outside the window and two blue jays speared earthworms from the ditch bank just beyond. She applied the red gloss to her lips, then sat with her hands folded before her on the kitchen table, seeing nothing, and waited for her husband.

"Get your coat," Buzz Newcomb said, allowing the screen door to slam behind him. She glanced his elongated shadow moving up the hall toward the bedroom.

"Buzz," she said, "why don't we just lie down for a little while?"

She drew a deep breath. Her husband's form filled the doorway, his whole body seeming to expand and contract like a huge lung. "Getcha damn coat," he said, and she saw the gun, hanging low like an extension of his own hand.

In the car, they drove past dead tobacco fields, stalks like stalagmites, stripped of leaves, silhouetted against the bruised October sunset.

Neither spoke. Buzz stared wide-eyed straight ahead, hunched over the wheel in eagerness and anger. Her talking would only make it worse now. Over the telephone, Gale had explained everything to Buzz, how it had happened. She was afraid to leave out anything. Now she could see him playing her words over and over in his head, putting an inflection here, a pause there, so that she had no idea what he was seeing. Everything she told him was true and exactly as it had happened—how she had met a man driving a pickup as she headed into town, how he'd waved and she'd waved just as folks do, how she'd glanced into her mirror and seen his truck making a U-turn, how he had parked beside her at the dentist's office.

They drove past the county hospital and merged onto the by-pass. Half a county to cover, she thought, time enough for him to consider what damage could be done and who could suffer it. When he stopped at the last light off the highway, she wanted to open the door and start walking in any direction other than the one they took.

Three hours earlier she had experienced for the first time the brute power a man could apply to a woman, comprehended fully how a man possessed the strength to twist a woman's arms off at the shoulder, force her thighs apart. A man had conveyed that force to her through a sinister smile and in the tips of his stained fingers when they touched her hand. "I know where you live," he had whispered in his whiskey breath. And now a second man was going to make him pay for it, only the bill was going to be hers.

When she'd picked up the phone to call her husband, Gale didn't think she could feel more afraid. The man's voice had wormed its way inside her: "I know where you live," he said. Raw fear possessed her. She had wanted safety, protection. She had gotten this.

Nobody would say that she and Mitchell Watford had ever been sweethearts, not even Buzz. The fact is their relationship, if it could be called that, had barely covered the months of June, July, and August those many years ago. To any observer, theirs would have been only one of a dozen high school summer flings. Gale was fifteen then, Mitchell was eighteen, a senior.

She lay on a towel in the hot sun that Saturday at Wildlife Lake and watched his long, even, effortless strokes as he swam across the lake and back again. She had willed him to look at her on his approach. The length of him rose from the water, his fingers raking back his coal black hair, his thick chest glimmering. He turned toward the shore, and she felt for the first time the full exercise of her feminine will.

He offered her a ride home in his new convertible, a black Firebird. She accepted. Everyone turned to watch as he unwound the towel that covered her white swimsuit, folded the towel over the hot black leather seat, and reached for her hand. At ninety miles an hour, Gale clenched the edge of the leather and closed her eyes as the sun and the hot wind pierced her thin swimsuit in the afternoon heat. He was eighteen, and she felt new all over.

It had been a short, hot summer. In September, she returned to New Hope High. Mitchell worked full-time for his father, who owned a crossroads grocery store. That was that. Ten years had passed.

Buzz, who was a year younger than Gale, knew these things. They had all attended the same small, rural high school. Besides, the year following the Mitchell summer, Gale had dated other boys, boys whose names she couldn't remember now, even boys from Columbia, boys who had seen her with Mitchell that summer, seen her blonde hair flying about her cool face, eyes shut to the wind, as if that whirl of golden hair twisted and glided on the music blasting from the black convertible.

Mitchell had raised her currency among the other boys that summer, and she had raised his among the younger girls. Buzz, who fancied himself a lady's man, hadn't shown the slightest interest in Gale until word of her had somehow been validated by the Mitchell summer.

Mitchell Watford had disappeared from her life as quickly as he had entered it, taking none of her, she thought. Sure, sometimes she would hear a song from that summer or see a blonde girl in a black convertible. And perhaps during her first years of marriage those summer images flashed before her after Buzz had turned from her and instantly fallen asleep. But whenever she thought of him at all in the months and years that followed, Mitchell's memory was adorned with the quality of dreams. She recreated him as it suited her, dressing him in shirts he'd never worn, taking him places they'd never been.

She had married Buzz and moved across the county. They had no mutual friends or common interests. He had simply disappeared. She had forgotten about him completely.

The small rectangular highway sign said Pharaoh, two miles. When they reached the intersection, Buzz slowed, then ran the stop sign.

They crossed the bridge at Falling Creek and rounded a sharp curve. Ahead, black tire marks preceded the splintered leg of a sign for The Risqué Café, a topless video poker bar on the interstate.

At her five-year class reunion, Gale had sat alone folding and unfolding a paper cockatoo. Buzz, who had always been a little vain about his dancing, was on the dance floor, approximating his best Travolta moves. The paper bird-of-paradise she held served as the place card for the tropical theme. Gale sat and watched her former classmates, attempting to put names to the fading faces.

After a time, she found herself crossing the room for punch she didn't really want in order to read the name of a blonde woman who had come alone. The woman had appeared like a stranded traveler. Gale watched as she peeled away from the clusters of classmates that formed and unfolded.

Sharon Watford. Gale read the name again, and then remembered. She was the daughter of the local highway patrolman, the fragile bird-like girl who had shouldered the blame whenever a classmate got a speeding ticket.

The DJ fired up "Stayin' Alive" and the tables emptied. Buzz did his Broadway-on-his-knees slide up to a former cheerleader's chair. Everyone at the table clapped, and the blushing cheerleader stood and took his hand.

Later in the night, as someone passed around a bottle, Gale overheard Buzz laughing with a hunting partner, repeating the rumor that Mitchell Watford had lost his father's grocery store in a poker game, and then the connection was complete. Mitchell had married a blonde-haired girl from Gale's class who had been deeply in love with him before Mitchell ever knew the girl was alive.

Two or three years later, Gale had read a single line in *The News and Press* reporting that Mitchell had been arrested for drunk driving. But she made no connection between that name and the boy with coal black hair and ice blue eyes who had relieved her of her beach towel and pointed with a fetching smile at the speedometer when the red needle rested on 100. He certainly was not the one who, that dream summer, had unbuttoned her blouse and kissed her neck, and who had later sat back against the opposite door with his own shirt open and the full light of the moon shining down on her. He was not the one who had demanded that she open her eyes and look down at her own nakedness in that light—not the possessor of the voice who had whispered to her that her fingers were her own.

That was not the man who had stepped from the yellow state-owned pickup today and lumbered toward her, the beer-bellied figure with hollow colorless eyes. It was not the man from the moonlight who hours earlier had said to her with a broken smile that he had been looking for her house, that he knew now where she lived.

If she hadn't been so afraid, Gale would never have called her husband. But for a moment she *was* afraid, really afraid, and in that moment she had reached for the telephone. And now there was no way she could undo what was about to happen.

The pistol rested on the seat between them, as innocent and unknowing as a retarded child.

Gale saw the dirty yellow pickup parked in the drive a quarter mile ahead. For a few seconds she had convinced herself that the truck wouldn't be there, that Mitchell wasn't a man who had a home, that he lived in bars, slept in that truck in the lot outside The Paradise Lounge. Now she looked at the man she had married. "Please," she whispered and waited. But he didn't answer.

Buzz shut off the engine. The house was a small, faceless brick structure with no porch, just two brick steps leading to the front door. White metal shutters stood on each side of the only window. Buzz softly closed the station wagon door. His eyes slowly, deliberately panned the freshly mowed backyard. He turned and carefully tucked the pistol between his belt and the small of his back, then moved quietly around the car to Gale's door.

"Wipe off that lipstick and get out," he said with the soft firm tone he'd use with a bird dog. Gale closed her eyes, lowered her head.

"No, no, no," she murmured. Buzz took one step toward her and spoke in that same soft voice.

"Get out now."

Gale opened the door. Buzz waited for her, then extended his hand, but she held back a step before following him to the front of the small house. She lifted a toppled tricycle left near the door and set it upright. Buzz gave the door three measured knocks.

Sharon Watford looked down without recognition at the couple at the foot of the steps. Bill collectors often came at suppertime. She didn't speak. She stood tall and waiting. Her thin limbs were pecan brown and dry, and although she was far along pregnant the skin on her face was so tightly drawn that she seemed to be facing a great wind. Her thin blonde hair hung straight down to her shoulders, too long and straight for a woman of her age and condition, and her immobile lips seemed translucently vacant of blood. One hand moved instinctively for the door handle, the other to her bulbous stomach. She just looked at them, her dark, deep-set eyes fierce against the man and woman at her door.

"I'm sorry to take you from your supper," Buzz said softly. "I'm here to see your husband."

The scraping sound of a kitchen chair ushered from behind her, and a small, blonde boy of about two ran tottering toward the pregnant woman and wrapped both arms around her leg. She lifted the child without taking her eyes from Buzz and Gale, then retreated one step back from the door.

"I promise this will only take a minute," Buzz said in that same soft lyrical voice as he opened the screen and stepped inside. He stood almost apologetically, his arms loose, his head tilted slightly in deference to the woman. Sharon glanced back over her shoulder and stepped aside.

Behind her, filling the kitchen doorway, Mitchell Watford wore a black sleeveless tee shirt that barely covered his belly. The black hair covering his arms, shoulders, and neck formed a kind of shadow around him. He didn't speak, just looked down at the white paper napkin he wiped his hands in.

Buzz stepped toward Mitchell, then looked back at his wife, his eyes dragging her inside. Gale entered the room, stopping a few feet behind her husband, who waited ceremoniously for her to take her place beside him. Sharon's wide, savage, jealous eyes raked up and down the length of her. And in that instant she felt the pregnant woman transforming her flesh into the flesh of every woman Sharon had long imagined and angrily feared. Gale turned her eyes away, feeling at once naked and betrayed.

Buzz spoke without emotion to the man standing across the small room from him. "I'm going to ask you just one question, and you are going to answer yes to that question. And then this will be all over and I will go back home and have myself some supper. You're gonna say yes and then this will be over."

Sharon looked back at her husband now. The child in her arms reached for her face and attempted to force her eyes to his, then sensing failure, looked at his father. Gale's eyes shot from Buzz over to Mitchell—who glanced up at her, then out the window to his left, then back down to the paper napkin in his hand. He pulled at the napkin, forming small white wings. Gale wanted to stop it.

"Buzz," she pleaded.

"Look at me," Buzz said to the other man, moving his hands behind him, lifting himself to his full mental height, finding the pistol's grip.

"Oh, Jesus, Buzz, oh Jesus," Gale murmured.

"You do understand don't you–" Buzz paused until Mitchell slowly lifted his eyes–"that if you ever even *look* at my wife again, you're a dead man?"

Mitchell's eyes studied the white wad of paper napkin, which rested in one hand, then passed it to the other, slowly, as if he were judging its weight. The remaining light from the afternoon seemed to drain from the room, leaving dull red particles of dust floating in from the open door and window. For a moment the white napkin appeared to glow, its light trailing from hand to hand like a tiny, fluttering white bird.

"It is a yes or no question," Buzz said in that Sunday school voice. His hand gripped the pistol. He lifted it slightly.

A deep surge in her belly made Gale shut her eyes to keep from vomiting. *She saw the pistol, felt the concussion of its blast, smelled the hot blood and flesh, heard the baby's one-note scream.* A tremor rushed up her body, and when it reached her eyes they flew open with a start.

Mitchell was looking at her with that crooked smile, with those distant, accusing, triumphant eyes. And Buzz, who had seen that look and knew instinctively its message, turned in wide-eyed disbelief from Gale Newcomb to Mitchell and then back to his wife.

Mitchell's eyes shifted without expression to Sharon, who stared vacantly at the floor, as if it went down forever. Again he trained those dark, knowing eyes on Gale, then guided them slowly and deliberately to Buzz, where they came to rest. The pistol had nearly cleared his belt before Gale could grab Buzz's arm.

"This is all a misunderstanding," Gale said in a breathless gasp. She was looking at Sharon now. "This–all of this–is just a mistake, Buzz. Nothing happened. Listen to me, nothing happened." She gripped Buzz's arm with all her strength, felt him trembling.

Mitchell turned his eyes on Gale and raised his lip again in that broken smile he'd given her earlier, a chilling look of conquest or collusion, which he next brought down on her husband.

"Listen to your wife," Mitchell said, his voice cracked and hard. "She's probably got some things to tell you, son." He again turned that smile on Gale, who could only think of the killing she couldn't stop.

"Mitch?" All eyes turned to Sharon, who looked down toward a bottom she couldn't see. "Mitch? You've got to come clean. You can do it now or you can do it before the Lord, Mitch. But you got to come clean. For once you got to come clean. It might as well be now." She stroked the baby, who had fallen asleep. The room was dark, except for the kitchen light. Each silent second fell upon the previous one, until the compression of soundlessness filled the small room. A breeze rushed through the screen door, and a dissonant, growling rumble slowly ascended from the metal spring holding the door shut. The smell of freshly cut lawn filled the room. Mitchell shifted from one foot to the other, and his shadow fell over his wife.

"You just might be a lot closer to the Lord than you think, pal," Buzz said, allowing his anger to show for the first time.

Mitchell squeezed the napkin into his palm and looked up, his expression unchanged. "A man has to listen to his wife, I reckon. A wife could tell her husband a thing or two, I suspect," he said and waited for the words to sink in. "Things he never knew." He dropped the crushed napkin. "Yes, sometimes a wife knows things." Mitchell nodded toward Gale. "Sometimes mistakes is made—like she said."

For a very long time they were the only five people alive, dark figures standing alone without sound or movement or light, not even hearing their own breathing.

"Then we all understand each other?" Buzz said in a thin voice, sliding the pistol back down into his belt.

Mitchell spoke only to Gale, his voice clothed in darkness. "I think you could say that. Yes, I think everything is clear now."

Sharon stood like granite, the sleeping boy against her side, her head bowed, her eyes closed.

A pale green light from the gauges and speedometer illuminated the face of the man and his wife. The eyes of both seemed fixed on the white dashes of the centerline in the headlights. Buzz reached for the pistol on the seat and laid it gently on the dash above the speedometer. Gale turned toward the darkness outside her window.

The outline of vine-choked tobacco barns appeared and disappeared and she thought of a time when she was twelve years old, when a boy from Pharoah, who was fourteen, led her to an abandoned tobacco barn on a night like this one, warm and damp in October. He carried a .22 rifle and a flashlight. The smell of baked earth and pinesap filled the inside of the barn, and small dust clouds rose like smoke when they stepped inside. He showed her where to point the flashlight, where they would likely nest or perch. And she saw at once that the tiny birds were blinded by the flashlight's sharp beam and that the killing was easy. She held the light and he did the shooting. After a time, she reached for the rifle and felt for the first time the ease of its smooth trigger.

"Take down your window," Buzz said.

"Huh?"

Buzz was rolling his window down. "It's warm out. This may be our last warm night of the year." He let up on the gas so that her hair didn't blow in her face. He patted the seat where the pistol had been. "Sit here," he said, "and talk to me."

Gale turned away from him. In her mind she had been some place she knew well, in a different night, and now she couldn't remember where her thoughts had taken her.

Buzz sighed, then looked from his wife to the road, then back at his wife. "Put on some lipstick and talk to me," he said, feeling down to the floorboard and lifting her purse. She didn't answer. He reached for the visor above Gale's head and jerked it down with force enough to free its spring-loaded, lighted mirror. "Put on some goddamned lipstick, I said." She reached into her bag. Buzz glanced over as she glossed her lips, then pushed up the visor. She dropped the lipstick into her bag and turned away from him.

Buzz pressed the gas hard and the car surged into the night. The wind lifted Gale's hair, whipping her cheeks and eyes. A low sound like the lid of a pot coming to boil began to rise as the car gained speed and the white dashes from the horizon became a single unbroken line. The boiling metal sound intensified as the revolver vibrated against the windshield. As if delivering a jab, Buzz jerked down the visor. Its soft light fell once again on Gale's face. "Look," he shouted. "Look at those goddamned red lips. I said LOOK!" Gale turned her eyes up into the mirror. Her blonde hair whipped her cheeks, flying left and right in a wild, electric dance, stinging her face. She was all red lips and frantic, blonde hair. The red speedometer arrow neared ninety, and the car began to rise and softly fall, like sleep breathing. Buzz was shouting now over the wind and the revolver, the warm wind of 100 miles an hour blowing the side of his face to distortion, his neck veins thick and blue.

"You want me to beg you for it, don't you?" he screamed. The deep woods were all around them now, like a tunnel or a cave. "You want me to beg you like a *dog*."

Someone To Crawl Back To
William Chapel Reynolds and Gale Newcomb

Wallace's drive-in was a beer joint called the Starlite Restaurant. And most nights Wallace and I sat outside under its rusting neon sign and drank and talked about the things that neither of us could say to other people. We'd smoke cigarettes and look up at what was left of the sign and say whatever it was we had to say.

The Starlite sign, even now, is the tallest one in the county. It was the pride of Darlington in the early sixties when Wallace's parents built the place, and teenagers from Hartsville and Florence came to the drive-in to hear the music blast from big horn speakers mounted on the roof, and to kiss and make-out in their cars.

The letters on the sign, the ones that hadn't burned out, arched over Wallace and me late at night. The soft blue and red neon colors gave us what light we needed to pour our drinks without spilling, and to light our cigarettes with dignity, and to say what needed to be said. The "i" in STARLITE was dotted by a spraying comet, if you can picture that, and all the letters in RESTAURANT were burned out, except for a couple of A's, a U, and an R. And it was between their soft red and blue light that we drank and talked.

Sometimes when it was really late and I was about to pass out, I'd be aware of myself, almost as if I was outside myself, watching.

I know that sounds crazy, but that's what happens when I know I'm about to go under. I see myself–like at the very end of a movie as the camera slowly pulls back–staring up at the STARLITE AURA with the black night behind it and the real stars way off. I feel myself lifted up. Then I'm gone.

Wallace said he was pretty sure I wouldn't die in Florida.

"Human flesh," he said softly, "is tougher than lettuce leaves and grapefruit rind." The smoke from his cigarette drifted above his eyes. "Shoot, Chapel, you'll have all summer to save for winter." He was looking up, talking at the sign. I could see the comet reflected in his eyes. "Hell, when was the last time you heard of anybody freezing in Florida? Never happens." He thumped the filter of his cigarette to the side and passed me another beer. "If things get too bad, look up the guy with the bum colony."

"Look up where?"

"He's famous all over Florida," Wallace said. "Never wears shoes. All the bums know him." For a second, his eyes went blank, staring out into nothing, going off. Then he was back.

"Start with tourist places," he said. "Try the dog tracks." He offered me a light. "You could probably find a bartending job." Neither of us said anything. "I'll give you the names of some people," he said finally. I took a long, hard pull on my cigarette. It wasn't likely anybody on Wallace's list would have an address.

Not that I had much choice about staying. A deputy making the rounds had paid a visit to the drive-in earlier in the afternoon equipped with a bench warrant with my name on it. Over the past six months, I'd run out of money before I'd run out of checks. So just to balance everything out, I'd kept writing until the checks were all gone, too.

Everything was just a matter of time.

"I've got some business to take care of," I said, looking up at the soft red and blue lights. "I got to get some things worked out before I go."

"What you got to do is haul your ass out of this town while you still got an ass to haul. You go fooling around, the *best* thing can happen to you is the sheriff finds you before somebody else does." I could feel him looking at me, waiting for me to read his expression, but I just looked out at the stars. He tapped his aluminum leg with his empty beer can and waited for me to say something—which was his way of letting me know that acting like I was wasn't working.

After he was shipped home from Vietnam, Wallace settled in Key West. He'd been sent back with one less leg than he'd gone over with, and he didn't want to live here where everybody'd known him when he was whole. He wouldn't have come back to Darlington at all, he'd said, except that after his parents died there was nobody to see after the Starlite or send him money. The fact is, I learned when Wallace and I had got to be friends enough to talk, that he'd gone so far down in the bottle he was afraid he was going to die. "Be careful what you wish for," he'd said. He also told me once, and only once—and this when we were about as drunk as we could ever get—that while he was in Florida and drinking at his worst, there had been some trouble and he'd killed another bum, that that was the real reason he'd come back to Darlington.

"What you studying about there, Chapel?" he said. "Looks like you're going off there, Bo."

"Just thinking about Florida. You know, bikinis and the smell of suntan oil."

"Right. Well, you can forget about the good-byes to the business you got to take care of. She don't need no more bruises on account of you."

"Oh, don't say it, Wallace, you want the ring back."

"You know what I'm saying." He was leaning in toward me now. I wasn't looking at him. I couldn't.

"Hell," I said, "I've decided you're giving up this old beer joint and going with me to Florida. We'll start something there."

"We'll start something all right." Wallace was kind of bearing down on me now. "If you don't get your ass outta here tonight, Chapel, somebody's liable to cut you into pieces so little even Florida gators wouldn't have you. You hear me?"

"I just got some things to do," I said. "Then we'll be gone."

I could feel Wallace looking at me.

The thing about a real friend is that when you lie to them they know it and you know it, and sometimes that's a way to say things in the most truthful way. I promised Wallace that I'd have his pickup back to him at the Starlite by the time the cleaning crew was done, around four in the morning. I told him that I had a few things to take care of, that I had to pack my bags, that I wouldn't see Gale. And he knew of course I was lying.

"Here," he said, handing me two twenties and nodding toward his pickup, "I think it's empty." I took the money and his keys. Wallace was looking up at the red and blue sign, or out beyond it, holding his beer up to it like a champagne toast when I drove away.

The tank was full. I broke one of the twenties at the Sav-Way for a six-pack, drove country roads from Stoney Creek to Pharaoh and back to Darlington again, thinking the whole time about how to tell Gale I was leaving. It wasn't going to be easy. There was no way I could take her with me. Things had gotten to that point. But then things hadn't gotten to the point where I could leave without her, either. That was where I was. There was no future with her, none without her.

I tossed my empty can out the window and felt for a cold one. When I glanced up at the stars, I thought of Gale's eyes. I could see the way her eyes crinkled when she smiled, could hear her voice when we'd sing to the radio together, and then I remembered a story she told me when we were so much in love we didn't care about anything else. This is it. She said this to me last Christmas Eve. She had married Buzz, she said, because she'd given up on ever really loving anybody. For years she'd had conversations with God about why He had never sent her the right man, and finally, after she'd gotten no sign from above, she'd married him. She started crying with the saddest eyes I've ever seen, funeral eyes. I remember it like it was yesterday, those eyes. I had a car then. We were parked at the K-mart, right next to the side of the building, out of sight. It was raining hard, and we sat quietly with the headlights off and the engine running, and for a minute or two she stopped crying. When it started up again, she turned away from me, crying so hard her words lurched out like a little girl's, and she caught her breath and choked out that she had failed God, and Buzz, and me, too, because she had not waited for me to come. She had not waited like she should have, she said. If she just had another chance, she said. If she could just undo everything, she said. Now if you have ever loved and been loved by a woman like that, you don't just skip town. You can't live with yourself if you do.

"Do you know what time it is, Chapel?" She'd answered on the fourth ring. I could tell she'd been sleeping.

"I've got to go. I'm going tonight, baby." There was a long empty time. I was standing at the pay phone outside the Food Lion. The place looked twice as big with nobody inside and the lights way down. "Gale?" I said finally. There was another long empty time, then a heavy, hurting sigh on the other end. "You know I love you," I said. "Don't you?"

"Make me a promise, if you really do love me, Chapel," she said. "I don't care what it is, Chapel, just make me one, okay? Tell me that you're never gonna see me again. It don't matter what you say. It don't. All that matters is that it is a true promise, you know, something that can't be broken without consequences. Something you have to pay for if you lie, Chapel. Something that's not a lie.

"I'm coming to pick you up," I heard myself say. "We're going to Florida. Tonight."

I had several hours to kill. Buzz would be in from his UPS Charlotte run around two. He'd be asleep by three. She'd have her suitcase packed and hid in the front closet. She said she had to leave Buzz a note. And so I made her promise she wouldn't give him a hint that we were going to Florida. Then she'd walk to the end of the dirt road with her suitcase and meet me at the highway. She waited for me to promise I'd be there at the highway by 3:45, said she loved me in a voice that made my heart stop, and then hung up the phone.

A spooky feeling came over me as soon as I hung up and started back to the truck, like I was being watched. I turned around and looked up. The dark grocery store lion was right over my head. It was a giant, like something at the pyramids. Some signs aren't meant to be seen so close up and without light. I just stood there, studying it. It didn't look like a lion at all. What it looked like was a big dog, with a .45 stuck in his mouth.

The radio was up loud. I looked down at the speedometer resting on 70, then over at the last two beers. I didn't want to get too drunk, so I spaced them out by time. I gave them twenty minutes each. That's how long it would take me to hit I-95 at Dillon and drive the twenty miles north to the Risqué Cafe, a titty bar with video poker machines on the interstate, exactly half way between New York and Florida. Wallace and I had gone there when the place first opened. I remember Wallace pointing out the license plates from all over America, which is why I wanted to be there, in another county, surrounded by people going and coming, where nobody knew me.

I opened the next-to-last beer, and by the time I was nearly done with it I was thinking of Gale. Suddenly, I was lifted up. Rounding a long, graceful curve in the darkness, I felt a warm breeze, the kind you feel at some time every spring, one that announces to you, this is it, no more surprising cold spells, no turning back now. It is the first breeze of summer, and you feel it, and come, in that instant, to know it surely, and a certain feeling goes through you. Like a flash, that good feeling mingled with what I was feeling for Gale, and I knew everything was going to be all right. Everything was going to be different.

The lot outside the Risqué Cafe was half empty, cars and trucks from all over were parked like dogs who'd just found a spot and dropped down. I pulled to the back corner, right next to the building where it was darkest, shut off the lights and the engine. A steady thumping from the music inside rattled a beer can somebody'd left on a window ledge above where I sat in Wallace's pickup. I put the twenty under the floor mat so I wouldn't be tempted and counted what was left, a ten, four ones and some change. I felt around under the seat and found enough silver to give me fifteen to carry in. The twenty under the mat would buy us a tank of gas, which, with what was left in the tank, would get Gale and me over the Florida line.

I'm a pretty good poker player. The key is to know when to quit. And to learn every way there is to cheat, and when to cheat and when not to. After Wallace and I first got to be friends, we'd go down to Myrtle Beach and find a game with some insurance-selling golfers. We never let on that we knew one another. We'd drink and lose some money, and let the insurance guys think we were stupid rednecks. You can guess the rest. Our plan was that if anybody caught us cheating, I'd pull out my knife and go for Wallace. You should have seen their eyes big as hubcaps when I'd dive for Wallace and the knife'd strike the aluminum leg.

My plan now was not to drink, but to watch the poker machines for a while, to wait for one that had been fed a good bit, then to take it first chance I got. I'd play three five-dollar hands, and see what happened. I couldn't see that it would make much difference if I lost, not in the long run. And if I won, it could make a hell of a difference. If I lost, I'd move around the bar, watch the titty dancing until the waitress took my two-drink-minimum order, then I'd stroll out while she went to the bar. I had some time to kill. I'd sober up some before I picked up Gale.

As soon as I walked in, the music stopped. The bar was right up front, and the poker machines were on my left against the wall. The empty bar, which seated maybe ten, was lit only by red and blue neon beer signs. Individual lamps hung over each of the poker machines so that the bartender could keep an eye on them. The players, who sat hunched over in the little tent lights, looked like they were praying in the Light of God. I couldn't see the stage in the other room, just the faces of the men there, all covered in red light. The loud music started again, and the wall that separated the bar from the rest vibrated with every drumbeat.

"What can I get you?"   The bartender was talking to me but looking over at one of the machines.

"Draft," I said.   He reached for a mug without ever taking his eyes from the machines.   I laid two-fifty on the bar.   Two beers and two five-dollar hands, I thought.   I couldn't see how it would make much difference, not in the long run.   Besides, I was thirsty all of a sudden.   I picked up the beer and turned to watch the players.   The bartender sort of hovered over me, thinking, I guess, that I was going to leave him a tip.   When he saw I wasn't, he raked the money into his palm and left me alone.

A thin, white-haired guy in a Dixie Cup jacket with three empty glasses on his machine turned to order another drink, but nobody saw him.   The old guy wore a neat, thin white beard, and his eyes were so pale and blue that he looked a little spooky.   He tore the plastic from a cigar, glanced over at me, and counted the few bills next to his hand.   I strolled over to the doorway near the dancing, where I could watch the women and wait on the old man.   I was already nearly done with the beer.

The dancer had short, shiny black hair and the thin body of a little girl.   There was something about her eyes when she smiled.   She had the littlest titties I'd ever seen on a dancer, but her eyes were really pretty, so pretty that I watched her face more than her tits.   There were four tables off the side of the stage with young guys, maybe in their twenties.   One of them, I figured out soon enough, was about to get married.   Most of the other tables had a guy solo.   The young ones were whooping it up, and after the first song they stood in line to toss money on the dance floor.

While I was watching the party, the old guy at the machine had ordered another drink and was almost done with it when I looked back at him.   A young bouncer-looking guy with short Brillo hair, and a woman with lacquered skin sat at the bar.   They both had real dark tans, but they didn't look too happy.   You could see in their shrink-wrapped faces and in the way they sat–together but not together–that they'd been fighting.   He stared straight ahead, rubbing his forearm like he'd been bit, and she tilted her head away from him and blew her cigarette smoke like it was made of cuss words.

The girl danced two more songs, and half-way through the second one she flipped off the G-string.   I saw her little naked behind.   She danced up a step or two toward the party of young smiley men.   Three of the young guys snared the one who was to be married and dragged him to the stage. They were all laughing, and the groom looked back at the others who were clapping and laughing at the tables and didn't put up much of a struggle. When he got to the stage, the others pressed his shoulders and he went down on his knees.

"Get used to it," one of them shouted, laughing.

The girl danced in slowly toward him. I could see all of the guys' smiling faces. Then, when she was a step away, she turned her back to them, facing me. The way she had shaved, she really did look like a little girl. I saw her face again. She was just a child. She leaned forward with her hands on her knees, took a step back, and wiggled her ass when his mouth touched. I couldn't watch.

The blackjack machine the old man had held was empty. I laid my cigarettes on it to hold my place and went to the bar for a beer. The tanned muscle-guy stood up from his stool as I walked over, and just as he turned away from her, the woman spoke in his direction.

"You better save me some," she said. The man didn't pay her any mind as he headed for the door.

I guess because I don't tip the bartender, he stands off pretending I wasn't there. The music stops again, and the woman taps her glass on the bar. She orders a gold tequila, two lemons. When it comes, she takes out her green gum, positions it on the corner of her napkin beside her drink. She looks down at the tequila in a way I recognize, and I think—as I watch her think—that she's gonna take a breath, run her fingers through her hair and throw back the shot. But she doesn't. The hair is the color of butter mixed in molasses, starched back like she's spent her life in a wind tunnel that has rounded out her cheeks, sloped her throat like a lizard's. She's a coke whore. She studies the tequila, then takes it down in four visits while I wait for my beer.

I feed in five bucks. I draw trash. I think about it, which is always my downfall, and figure I'll be lucky if I break even. Which I don't. I look down and see that my beer is gone, downed in one swallow when I didn't even know it, which doesn't seem right. So I'm thinking I'll get another beer and play a two-dollar hand, take it from there, for whatever it's worth. Then I look at my watch and think of Gale. I feed in the last five bucks, win seven-fifty on the five, lose it all in the next two hands.

The twenty is right where I left it, under the floor mat of Wallace's truck. My cigarettes and beer mug are on the machine to hold my place, but I trot back toward the entrance anyway on account of the bartender, who would like to piss in the pack, I think.

Out on the interstate, horns blow. When I look, I see the damnedest thing: This huge, skinny dog, a greyhound, I'd bet, is *walking* across the interstate. He never breaks stride. I'm thinking it's a miracle if he don't get splattered. But he doesn't. I just stand there, not believing what I'm seeing.

When the dog disappears, I look up at the night sky. You can tell that it's cold up there, on account of how bright the stars are. Then I think about seeing those same stars from somewhere in Florida, with Gale lying beside me, you know, seeing those stars reflecting in her eyes, and that feeling I had driving runs through me again.

The leather-skin couple are huddled in serious conversation when I come back in. And if the bartender ever knew I'd left, he doesn't let on. My cigarettes are right where I put them. I break the twenty for a beer. One of the fives I get back in change is brand new, and the machine takes it in like liquid.

God looks down on us.

I play Pot-A-Gold for the five bucks, and what I draw is a royal flush, and what it pays is $125. My heart does flips and spirals. Cash in, I think. I look at my watch. I can cash in, buy a six-pack to go, drive the speed limit, and be back to meet Gale at the highway with time to spare. Time to just pull over, have a beer and wait for her.

Or I can play high/low to double. I decide I'll cash in. Then I remember that I'm still holding two fives. I can have a drink and think about what to do. I backpedal toward the bar, watching the machine, not that there's anybody who's gonna steal my hand. I'm afraid there might be a power failure, you know, some act of God, and so I back toward the bar.

"Hey, hotshot, buy your friend a drink." It's the woman. The man has left again.

I look at the bartender, then back at the machine. "Can't do it," I say to the machine. "I'm on my way to Florida."

She sort of chokes, laughing and drawing at once on her cigarette. "W-e-l-l," she hacks, "they won't stop you at the state line, keep you from crossing for buying me a drink, now will they? I could do you some good in Florida."

I look over at her, and she's smiling.

.   "I got connections you wouldn't believe in Florida. I'm from Miami. Him and me," she motions toward the door, "we've been vacationing, to New York to do some business. But my connections are all over Florida. That's where I'm headed, too."

"I'll have a bourbon," I said.

"And I'll have another—on him," she said, pulling hard on her cigarette, sizing me up. I slid the other two fives toward the bartender. If I cashed out I wouldn't miss the ten. She was just holding the tequila, studying it, when my drink finally comes.

Facing me when I sat down, the words "Royal Flush $125" were lit up still. I rotated the drink slowly, icing it good, waiting for some sign. When none came, I lifted the glass. The bourbon was warm and cool at once. Well, I thought, am I high or am I low or am I a cash-out nothing. I heard the words go through my head in a sort of sing-song way, and I smiled at the sound, which made me think of Gale. "Am I high? Or am I low?" I sang. "Or am I a cash-out noth-ing?" I'm *high*, I thought, and with a slow graceful arch my finger pressed the High button.

And I was a winner. "Yes!" I yelled, turning and smiling at the bartender, who paid me no mind, and then at the couple, who smiled at me, and then at each other, then spoke to each other—then looked back at me.

When I tried to hand the pay-out slip to the bartender, he said I'd have to cash out with the manager, then turned his back. I walked around the end of the bar, where the Florida couple was huddled again, back through the wide door where the stage was. Three of the dancers were sitting at the young guys' tables. Their friend who was about to get married sat apart from the others, as if the party had tilted away from him, passed out with his mouth half open, wearing only his boxer shorts, looking like a broken piece of furniture. At the very back of the room in a corner, behind a fake tree, I saw the lighted outline of a door with an office sign. The bourbon and the excitement of winning made me a little wobbly, and I missed the door handle first try.

Before I could give it another shot, the manager, a rutty-faced guy with jet-black dyed hair and wearing an over-starched white shirt, pushed open the door. The little girl dancer sat across from him in a housecoat, staring at the floor. He took the cash-out slip from me, looked at the amount, then handed it back to me with a pen to sign. She didn't look up. She was in the principal's office, you could just tell. The man opened the desk drawer with a key, counted out five fifties, and handed them back over his shoulder for me to take, looking at her the whole time, waiting for what she didn't want to say, it seemed to me. She looked up with sad, puppy-like eyes.

I folded the money and started out. Gale would be waiting when

I got there. I'd get us a six-pack to ride on.

The Florida woman's head rested on the bar. Her eyes were closed. The burly guy signaled to me.

"Hey, gimme a hand, will ya, pal? Help me get her to the car."

I looked over at the bartender, who was reading a newspaper at the other end of the bar.

"Come-on, pal, just lift that side so she can walk. You never *even* seen a mean bitch till you seen this one ruin her new shoes." He was holding up one side of her. I took the other arm, and we lifted her. Her head lopped to the side as the three of us wobbled toward the door. Outside, she stepped softly off the curb. Hauling her took more effort than I'd expected. The work made my blood pump, made me a little weak-kneed from the liquor.

"Let's give her a breath of air," the man said. I looked up at the night and thought about the time.

"Look, I got to go, I got to be somewhere."

"Where're you parked?" he said.

"Round there." I motioned with my head.

"Good, me too," he said, hefting her up.

We made it around the dark corner and were near the back of the lot. A cold breeze stirred.

"Heavy bitch, ain't she? That one yours?" he said, nodding toward Wallace's truck.

"Yeah."

I felt her weight lift from my shoulder. I glanced over at her. She was staring wide and shiny-eyed at the man. Like an animal. Then I looked over at him. She pulled away from me.

"Well??" She was looking at him. "Well, what you waiting for, Brint? Do it, Brint, do it, do it you fuck!"

I don't remember feeling anything.

Then I was flying through black space so high and cold I couldn't stop shivering. A blowtorch roar filled my ears. There were dim lights far away and then bright flashes, like matches struck on my eyeballs.

Everything was dark. The blowtorch faded into the low rumble I knew was the sound of Wallace's truck.

I was in and out.

Thick, vise-grip hands took hold of my ankle and one wrist, and

I was dragged like a bag of fertilizer, sideways down the ribbed bed of the truck. My right ear folded back against my head, and with the thumping something warm ran from my nose or mouth, down under my folded-back ear.

The knuckles on my free hand raked chunks of gravel.

Blood flooded inside my head; I was suspended in air, weightless. Then falling. After I hit, I tumbled and flipped until I thought I'd never stop. The cold ground around me trembled.

Stinking, wet breath washed over the side of my face. The weight of the hot, sour air hurt my cheek and swollen-shut eye. Against the moonlight, I made out the thin snout of a black hound.

Way off somewhere, babies were crying.

Directly overhead, all was bright blue.

Out at the horizon, as far out as you could see, just above the water, the sky was deep red with streaks of thin clouds. Night was shaping up. Sandwiched between the coming night and the ending day, where the rotting dock curled down into the water, the sky was purple. Me and Wallace sat in the heavy shade, on what was left of the porch outside the shack, looking out on the Indian River. We sat in old pine rockers, drinking red wine from big, fancy silver cups, like from the time of the knights.

Wallace made Florida seem as close to paradise as I was likely to get. "Human flesh is tougher than lettuce leaves, tomato skins and grapefruit rind," he said, stroking the throat of a young black Labrador that kneeled beside his chair. The dog raised her muzzle, closed her eyes at his touch. Its whelp mate, resting beside me, suddenly raised his head, wide-eyed, ears high, alert.

"Watch them dogs," Wallace said. He took his hand from the female, and she raised her head like she'd received a message, heard some call. The wind picked up, gently blowing back their black manes, bringing in the smell of the river. The dogs sat stiff as tight muscle, looking out at the horizon like lion statues. For a time Wallace just looked out at the sun, which now was maybe two inches off the water. Way back, the sky was really red, above the broken dock a deeper purple. I watched the dogs, waiting.

Then, at the same instant, the two Labs sprang to their feet and pressed their faces into the wind, out toward the water. "Keep your eye on them dogs," Wallace whispered. I looked from the Labs out to the river. The shadows from the saw grass were long now and covered most of the yard between the porch and the dock. The wind was cool when it came from the land side, warm off the water. In a minute the two dogs began pacing around my chair in widening circles, like planets turned loose from the sun, gliding finally from one end of the porch to the other. It was clear something had them shook up.

Off to the left, seven bums were sitting in a line behind the tall grass at the river, watching the sun enter the water. In a minute, two more bums appeared from behind a shed and crossed the yard, leaving long shadows as they headed for the water line. They didn't speak.

"Are you ready, Chapel? Are you ready, son?" The two darted from side to side, ears up, their noses jutting into the cool breeze, suddenly sitting, then up again pacing, making little begging sounds. They coiled a path around us like water around stones. You'd have thought they were trapped on an island surrounded by rising tides. The female stopped beside me, intense and anxious. Her eyes–thick with water and red with reflection from the sinking sun–had fixed on something out there, maybe something in the sunlight, something I couldn't see.

"Hold on, Chapel," Wallace said softly. "It won't be long now." He nodded toward the water. The narrow shore was lined with drunks and bums, evenly spaced, sitting a few feet apart, Indian-style, each one facing out, alone. Three more were crossing the yard from the right, more in darkness than in light, and I saw the heads of two more bums rising from behind the sluice farther back. My hands and feet were cold, and I felt for my cup. You could see only the outline of the bums against the water and the red sky. I took a long drink from the silver wine cup, but when I set it down it somehow looked full again.

The two Labs lit off the porch as if they'd been fired from a slingshot, front legs extended half-again the length of their body, landing softly, then pulling so hard on the sandy gravel that their front paws folded into their hind parts, which dug in, sending them into the air again.

The narrow wooden dock dipped and curved from weather and rot, but the dogs make a straight black line down it, clearing the last plank, leaping toward the sun as if it were a flaming hoop. The female landed first, disappearing into the black water. I rose up from my seat, a little lightheaded.

Suddenly, the first young Lab erupted from the river, rising maybe five feet from the water like a movie scene run backward, folding, hanging frozen for a moment, then falling with a splash. Then the second dog cleared the water, sailed up as high as the first, folded, was held like a photograph by the last of the light, then fell back quietly into the water. When I looked again for the female, I saw the porpoise for the first time, saw it's snout lift the female under her front legs, send her up into the cool night, while the male swam toward it, eager to fly again.

I looked over at Wallace for some explanation. In the dim purple light, he looked like a very old man, the lines in his face deep and wide, his eyes fixed and sad. He didn't speak or move. And now the fading bums and drunks seemed to come from all directions and disappear into the shadows of the tall grass, an endless stream of them. In a few minutes it would be too dark to see the dogs playing, but I was sure somehow they would go on, flying up high, coming down like black question marks.

"This is the life, ain't it, Wallace?" I said. I couldn't see him in the darkness. In a moment the night would be done. The first stars appeared way up in the purple black sky.

"This is it, ain't it, Wallace? This is it."

You Can't Tell Me You Love Me Enough
Coach and BB

"What I do," said Coach lifting his beer, "is I aim for the center hole in the bottom of the urinal. As long as I'm on target, I'm okay." The Happy Hour men at the Paradise Lounge were discussing their personal, individual sobriety tests, how they determined if they were too drunk to drive home.

"Sometimes his aim ain't so good," said Coach's wife, BB, who was the new bartender. "Like most men, when he misses, he misses low," she said.

The other men at the bar laughed. One of the regulars, Pete, ordered a Royal Flush split three ways. BB poured the two liquors and juice into a chrome shaker, lined up three glasses, tilted the shaker over the glasses and waved it like a wand, pouring equal portions. She set a glass before Pete and Coach and held the third one up for a toast.

"Here's to love and crash landings–and to guys who can find the mark." Again the men laughed. In the year since she'd begun bartending, business had more than doubled.

"Damn, you're something, BB," Pete said to her. "Where does she come up with that stuff?" he said, looking at Coach. "If I could find me a woman like that, I'd give my ole lady the house, my truck, and my best hunting dog." The other men laughed. Pete lifted his glass, nodded to BB, and together they threw back their drinks.

Coach slid off the barstool, leaving the glass, reached back for his beer, then slowly walked over to the jukebox. He stood with his back to everything. He pressed the arrow button on the jukebox and looked at the shadow of his own reflection in the glass. The CD selections folded open like pages. He heard BB's voice, followed by another round of laughter.

"Play that slow Vince Gill song, would you, baby?" she called to him. Coach found the selection and fed a dollar into the machine, then pressed the buttons for the song. BB was telling a joke.

". . . and then the cop says, 'Okay, we'll help you find your car, mister, but you got to put that thing back in your pants', and the guy looks down and screams, 'They stole my girl, too!'"

Coach turned. BB tossed back the drink that he'd left on the bar as the men watched.

"Um, umm," she said, running the back of her hand over her mouth. "That's my song. You boys will have to fend for yourself while

I dance with the man I love."

She made a slinky path toward him as if she were in the center of a spotlight. Coach saw the looks on the men's faces. She put her arms around him and pulled him close, pressing her breasts against him, smiling at the men at the bar. She sighed deeply and closed her eyes. "Thank you, baby," she whispered. "I'll call you when I think I'm about done. Wait up for me?" Coach didn't answer. She was never insincere when she asked him to wait up, and she was never home when she said she'd be. "Hold me, baby," she said, pressing against his thigh. Coach closed his eyes and held her still for a second. He could smell the perfume she'd asked for. Opium, it was called. When he looked up again, every man at the bar was looking at her.

"It's getting too hot in here for me," Pete said when the song ended. He was standing beside his barstool holding open his wallet. He tossed two bills on the bar.

"If you want to know why I tip so good," he called to BB, "it's cause you're worth it." He shook hands all around.

"That'ed be half the phone bill," she whispered to Coach, then pushed away from him and walked back over to the bar.

"Thank you, Pete," BB said, scooping up the two tens.

"You welcome, Vivacious."

Coach watched from the patch of dance floor in front of the jukebox. BB laughed a little choked laugh and looked up at Pete. It was a look that fourteen years earlier had kept Coach awake at night, the look of a sixteen-year-old cheerleader in his History class who could read his mind and who told him so with that very look. It was no fake look, and not coyness either. It was seeing herself in your mirror.

Coach stood at the urinal in the toilet at the back of the bar. The sounds of jagged conversation, muffled music, and his wife's laughter rose and fell like distant surf from the other side of the door.

He raised his hand to check the time, and his eyes came to rest on the V-shaped scar on his middle knuckle.

After two years the thought of that single blow still sent an amphetamine rush through him. The image was as clear as assassination footage replayed a thousand times before his eyes: *the jerky, puppet-like rhythm in the kid's shoulders and wrist, the body bent forward at the waist, the head waving from side to side, the finger pointed into his face, the intimidation factor as practiced and perfected as a beautifully timed pass play—"You can kiss my mu-tha-fuckin'ass"—and the light spray of spit.*

And then that frozen instant of realization in the kid's eyes when Coach's fist landed and the kid's blood and teeth covered his knuckles.

He had pushed aside images of the bandit lawyers and the ambitious judge, the kid's weeping mother at the trial. Despite the thousand tiny disappointments he'd seen in BB's face over the past two years, that moment of savage satisfaction and exhilaration was solid and fixed.

Coach waited at the end of the bar to say good-bye while his wife blended margaritas. The telephone rang. BB held the receiver between her shoulder and jaw as she poured. She smiled into the receiver, glanced over at Coach, then turned her back as she spoke. He lifted the six-pack in front of him and walked out to his truck. As he turned the key to the ignition, he looked up at her through the wide window. She was standing on the bar, inventorying the mini-bottles. He could see the eyes of the men working her over.

The acorns under his tires made popping sounds as he pulled the truck up the drive and into the yard of the small yellow house. Her bar money kept the house and the truck from the finance company. His minimum wage job at the garden and lawn shop went to pay the settlement, always would.

Coach opened the truck door and sat with his feet hanging free from the cab. He felt for another beer. The October sunset was streaked with red and purple daggers like inverted flames. He drank. The wind picked up and the smell of his youth—squirrel hunting and half a life of football seasons—made rapid, fleeting pictures in his mind.

He collected the mail, separated it—his and hers—and set it on the kitchen table. He didn't look at the bills anymore. BB still received three or four catalogs a day, ones for clothes and gifts, department stores up North and out West, specialty catalogs, and he always stacked them neatly for her. He knew that she liked looking at them when she got home late from work. To him they were a painful memory of their happiest years, when she drove the red Camaro convertible and they went out for good meals together; when she was all tanned and he had won a state championship and married the high school's former homecoming queen; when she had bought little surprises for him from exotic catalogs.

After she looked through them, she dropped them in the trash before coming to bed.

      Coach filled the sink with scalding hot water and liquid soap and eased in the dirty dishes. He folded the laundry from the dryer, gathered hangers from the floor where BB dressed and hung what needed hanging in her closet. He collected her half-full coffee cups and the clothes she'd stripped off the night before, stacked her dirty ashtrays, deposited the clothes in the washer, emptied the ashes in the trash, and put the dirty glass and cups in the dishwater. He turned on the radio, took a beer from the refrigerator and sat at the kitchen table watching the steam rise from the sink. It dawned on him that he spent more time cleaning up after his wife than he spent with her.

      He went in at eight, got off at five; she went in at three and got off at closing–whenever that was. He worked and she slept on Saturdays. On Sunday mornings they made love, and in the afternoon they drank together.

      On the nights after work when he couldn't stand it, he'd drive back to the Paradise Lounge and sit with the other men at the bar, drink, watch, and wait for BB to get off work. She parceled herself out among the customers. The longer he waited, the less there seemed of her. The later the hour, the more impossible it became for him to leave her there. Some mornings he was too tired or hungover to get out of bed. Lately, his boss at the garden shop had warned him about calling in sick.

      After finishing the dishes, Coach stripped the dirty sheets off the bed and put on clean, crisp, pleasant smelling ones. He made the tucks at the corners with military precision and creased the fold before arranging the pillows. The smell of the clean sheets crept inside him like a cold shadow.

      He sensed her growing power over him, her expanding sense of prerogative.

      Coach opened a beer and wandered slowly, circling from room to room. He switched on the TV in the small den, then walked out before the sound came up. He reached for the porch light, opened the front door, and stood looking up into the clear autumn night. He could smell the coldness coming. First frost, he thought.

      Inside the bathroom, he set his beer on the back of the toilet, took off his shirt and ran hot water. He shaved slowly, holding the razor under the steaming water after several strokes, watching the blade until it was clean, then lifting it to his face. He undressed, dropping his clothes in the plastic basket beside the washer. Maybe he could sleep. If he slept now, the night would be over and he would wake early. He would make coffee first thing, maybe even wake BB for a cup before he left for work.   Some mornings after he dressed he'd sit at her dressing table beside the bed and have his coffee while she slept.

He checked the front door making sure it was unlocked for her, switched off the TV, and stepped into the bedroom, to the bed with crisp, clean sheets, into the smell of her dressing table powder and Opium perfume.   He had smelled her perfume as he danced with her–as men watched her.

Topping the bridge on the interstate, Coach dimmed his headlights and saw the tall Paradise Lounge sign ahead.   He reached for the blinker, took the exit.   The lot was full.   Coach circled until he spotted a parking space in the steakhouse lot beside the lounge.   Another late closing for BB, another morning when he'd barely make it to work.   He pulled open the lounge door.

BB was at the far end, up on her toes, bent forward in half, way out over the bar, her elbows flat on its surface.   He couldn't see her from the shoulders up.   Three young, professional salesmen stood huddled tightly above her, their ties hanging low, nearly touching her face.   Everybody was watching.

Coach took a seat at the corner of the bar nearest the door.   He saw now that BB held something cradled in her hands.   Two of the young men exchanged looks, smiled and looked down again at BB's face.   Then she dropped what she was holding, a piece of paper Coach thought, pushed away from the three, turned her back and slowly shook her head from side to side.   The shining eyes of the three men watched her fingers slowly circle then caress the fashioned, wooden tap handle.   As she pulled the draft beer, BB tilted her head way back and made a wolf call, "Aoooooooooow!"   The men laughed.   "You put that thing away, you dirty boy," she called back to one of them.   The blonde man picked up the paper on the bar and, exchanging smiles with the other two, tucked it into his wallet.   Turning with the glass of beer, BB spotted Coach, and the smile left her face.

"Beer?"   She mouthed the word.

"Something brown," he said in a voice that made the three men turn and look.

They watched her dip the glass into the ice, open a mini-bottle and pour the bourbon.   They were waiting for her next reply.

BB set the bourbon in front of Coach.

"What was on that piece of paper?" he demanded in a voice that surprised him.

"It was a picture."

The three men were laying cash on the bar, watching BB, knowing what she'd seen.

"What is it," BB went on, "about a woman fucking a dog," her voice trailed off. "This is turning into the night from hell," she said. The men were walking toward the door, their eyes on BB as they came closer. The blonde one slid a small rectangular piece of paper on the bar between BB and Coach without breaking stride. The other two watched BB's reaction from the door. It was a gold-embossed business card. When Coach looked back, the men were gone. BB lifted the card, carried it to the far end of the bar, and glancing back at the door set it on top of the cash register.

Coach leaned forward until his head rested against his knuckles.

When he opened his eyes, Coach realized how deeply he'd been inside his own head. The narrow bar area was suddenly packed with men. Cigarette smoke hung like gray cirrus just above the blasting music and shouted conversations. He watched BB move up and down the length of the bar as if it were one long see-saw, picking up empty glasses and dirty ash trays, her eyes always in motion, every beer replaced with a fresh one before it was quite empty. She lifted his empty glass and set another bourbon on a new napkin in front of him.

"You looked asleep with your eyes open," she said. Then she worked her way to the other end of the bar. Coach had sucked his lip until now he tasted blood.

When he stepped up to the urinal, he recognized the face of one of his former quarterbacks, a kid whose name he'd forgotten. Hammer or Hatchet, a nickname his teammates had given him. Hatchet. Something about his throwing arm. When the guy recognized him, Coach would call him Hatchet. He'd like that. He was sure it was Hatchet. The man zipped his fly and reached for his beer. He looked down at the floor as he flushed.

"Hey, old man. In case you haven't figured it out, you're pissing on the floor," he said. He finished off the beer and dropped the glass beer bottle in the plastic barrel beside the door.

Coach's seat at the bar had been taken. The man who held it
looked somehow ageless, maybe sixty, but lean and tanned, with a well
trimmed white beard and the cheekbones and perfect nose of an actor.
His eyes were a soft blue, so pale they seemed to emit light in the dim
room.   The man looked up at Coach, who looked from him to the
bourbon on the bar.

"Yours?" the man said. "Thought someone maybe left the drink
to go dance." The old man stepped down from the stool. "Hey," he said,
studying Coach's face, "I know you." Coach took the stool and reached
for a cigarette.

Behind the old man, a couple who had occupied the adjacent
corner of the bar, stood to pay. The husband tunneled a path through the
crowd toward BB at the cash register.

"You can have this one," said the woman, motioning for the old
man to take her stool.

"Is it still warm?" the old man said with a mischievous smile.

"If you don't think so, you can ask my husband when he gets
back." She laughed.

The old man turned to Coach. "You have to love'em, don't
you." The old man took the seat. The husband re-joined his wife.
"Night folks," said the old man. Then he turned to get BB's attention.
"Uhm," he said, looking from BB over to Coach. "My, my, my. The
view from here is better anyway."

"That's my wife," Coach said, waiting for the old guy to look at
him. "Not some piece of meat." He could feel his pulse in his temples.

The old man looked down into his folded hands on the bar.

When BB saw the look in Coach's eyes, she dropped the wet rag
she held.

"I'll have a scotch on the rocks," the old man said to BB, "and
I'd like to buy my boy here–by way of apology–a bourbon whenever
he's ready."

BB gave Coach a precautionary look, then turned to make the
drink.

"It's a good thing you're here on a night like this, son," he said
to Coach, looking around at the crowded room. "She's something to
look at. That's why this place is packed. I've often thought about
opening my own place. Find myself some beautiful women to work it,
treat'em right, and rake in the money. You got beautiful women,
treat'em right, the customers will come."

"You a fucking genius, ain't you?" Coach said in a tired, low voice. He lifted his drink. "You fuckin' Sam Walton come to walk with Elvis, ain't you, you old fuck."

"You don't have to be a genius to figure that out," he chuckled, watching BB walk back toward him with his drink.

BB saw the look in her husband's eyes. "Please," she whispered to Coach.

"I'll have that bourbon now, courtesy of the son of god here, knower of all fucking things big and small."

BB turned slowly and walked away, glancing back over her shoulder.

"Must be hard for you to sit here night after night, huh?" said the old man tasting his drink. "I wouldn't do it if I were you."

"You about one breath away from having your sorry ass knocked off that stool, bub."

The old man looked down and didn't speak. BB placed the drink in front of Coach, then laid her hand against his face, until finally his eyes looked up to her. He could see the tears forming there, welling up, begging him.

"When you kiss me," she whispered, "you make the moon roove." It was a verbal miscue from long ago, from their private language.

He gently pushed her hand away, looked down at his drink and lifted it to his lips. He heard her sigh. Then she was gone.

"I know how you feel, son," said the old man apologetically.

"Tell me this," Coach said. "Are you just into getting your ass stomped, or what?"

"I worked second shift at Dixie Cup for over thirty years, from the time I graduated high school, three to eleven shift. My wife, she worked for a doctor. She wanted to *be* a doctor in high school."

BB was pouring shots.

"I knew she wanted to, you know, be with her friends sometimes, and I told her it was okay if she went with a group of her girlfriends dancing sometimes. I didn't see any harm in that at the time. I wanted her to be happy."

BB slid the shots forward, laid down the change, a stack of bills, beside the drinks. A man's hand from across the bar covered hers. When she looked up, a tall mustached man wearing a cowboy hat stood smiling at her.

Coach saw the look, knew instantly its meaning. BB whispered something to the man, turning her eyes away.

Coach saw her lips, her eyes.

The static roar that filled the bar turned white, was sucked from the room. Only the image of the tall, mustached man, the look on BB's face, and the old man's voice remained.

"I paid the price," the old man continued. "Still do." He lifted his drink. "Sometimes she didn't come home until one or two. I'd lay awake, then fake sleep when she came home. I could smell the after-shave of the men she'd danced with. I wanted her to be happy, but I couldn't take it after a while."

"Do I look like a fucking shrink?" Coach threw back his bourbon.

The old man gave a small, embarrassed laugh. "You want another drink?" He took a sip of his scotch. "It's loneliness that is the Devil, you know."

The cowboy followed BB up the bar. Coach could see the fucker's lips moving. He set down his glass and slid from the barstool.

The old man caught hold of his sleeve. Coach looked back at him with rising fury. "I told her no more going dancing." Coach looked down at the old man's hand on his sleeve. "And she agreed," he said softly. Coach looked again for the tall man. He had disappeared. BB was lighting a cigarette.

"Hey, bartender," Coach shouted. People turned and looked. "Hey bartender. Who do you have to fuck to get a drink around here?" Coach held his glass up over his head, kept holding it up until she stood in front of him. People were watching. She reached up for the glass, but he pulled it away.

"You can make me a drink, but first you have to fulfill this old cocksucker's final wish. He wants you to dance with him, before he heads for the happy fucking hunting grounds, don't you, you old fuck. He promises not to put his hands on you, don't you, shithead." Coach looked around again for the cowboy, who had vanished. "He just wants to feel your warm tits against him, just wants a little gentle grinding, before he makes for The Exit, don't you, Old Wise One?" He handed BB the glass. She was holding back the tears. "I'll play that slow Vince Gill song you like, okay babydoll?" The tears were streaming down. She turned and walked away.

Coach could feel the heat radiating from his body, a rising nausea boiling inside. He heard no sound in the room, saw only the shrinking image of his wife.

"It was a good thing my wife worked for a doctor," the old man muttered, his eyes looking down into his hands. "She was sick all the time, allergic to everything."

The old man's lips were moving, but Coach wasn't hearing him now. BB disappeared into the stockroom behind the door.

"You know every time I smell fresh cookies I think of her. I go for walks in the mall, and I'm thinking of nothing until I smell cookies.

If Coach hurried now, while she was in the stockroom, there might still be a chance.

"One night, I called and she didn't answer. Called again. No answer. Then again. I can't tell you what I was prepared to do to her when I left the plant that night. When I pulled into the drive, I saw that all the lights in the house were on. I was sure she wasn't there, that she'd left early, her not thinking that she wouldn't be home in time to turn them off before I got home. She'd made that mistake in her dancing days."

BB walked out of the stockroom hunched over a case of beer. Her face was hard. She bent over the cooler loading beer down into it. Men stood with their money, waiting. She didn't answer when they called for a drink.

"When I put the key in the door that night, I can't tell you what I was thinking. But when I opened it, the whole house smelled of oatmeal cookies. She'd left them on the table. I sat there eating cookies, wondering where my wife was, what she was doing, what was going to happen when she got home. By the time I come back to my senses, I hear the radio or what sounds like voices in our bedroom. I go back to shut it off. I don't expect to see anybody in our bed. And when I go to her, I stand there and look down at her. Folks say she was already dead."

Coach reached for his drink. Last call would be coming soon. He waited for the old man to finish his story. BB refused to look at him. He'd listen to what the old guy had to say now. Listen and not think. He looked over at his wife who only looked down into the dark cooler as she loaded in the beer. The old man didn't speak. He looked again at his wife, whose shoulders stooped over the cash drawer as she counted change. His eyes fell on the stack of business cards on top of the cash register. The old man didn't say anything.

Coach reached for his bourbon, hesitated. He laid the palm of his hand over the glass. He looked down at his drink and then at the hand that covered it. His pupils widened. And in the dim, recessed light, the scar seemed to rise from the knuckle–like a brand, or a blessing.

Rehab
Joshua Severance and William W. Mims

When you fall in love, nobody asks any questions. When you fall out, everybody wants to know why. Nobody needs any help with the former. Industries are built on the latter. We fall. We blindly stagger around. We rejoice in our terrified hearts. We wait and hope for better times, for the chance, if we are lucky, to fall again.

Falling out of love is a mystery. Or at least that is what I believe, what I keep saying. It is what I tell myself over and over when other feelings try to bully their way into my heart. I say over and over, I've done my damage, done my time. I pray. I believe.

What I know is that for people who have been married to addicts of one sort or another, liquor, or dope, or gambling, or food, or sex, or money, the answer to the failed relationship can roll off the tongue like "Amazing Grace." Don't get me wrong. They've lived through hell. But at least they have a word for it.

"I just couldn't live with that," they say. And it is true. As true as true can be. Addiction is a mysterious, unbearable thing. But then there are more mysterious than not mysterious things, I say. At least that is my experience. Addiction, the word I mean, has such an appealing sound, such a swing to it. Sound it out, if you're not an addict. Feel it form and spin out in your own voice–ad-dic-tion. And it sounds so final, too, such authority in it, so complete, as words are sometimes. It needs no further explanation. If you find the word, you no longer need look for the thing itself. Because you've got the word.

There are some mysteries, like falling out of love, that we don't have words for, no matter which side of the fall you land on. A guy doesn't have to be a drunk for his wife to fall out of love with him, I tell myself. It's not the liquor she walks out on. But most people want you to explain everything to them. I understand that. And when you say there are no words, they look at you as if they've been hoodwinked. They don't like that. It is the horse that shits in their parade. You are hiding something, they think. Which means to them that you are what went wrong. Even if it was your wife who fell out of love with you.

But try turning the situation around and you'll see how stupid their thinking is. Try this: Go out some lovely spring day to your neighborhood park. Find two people who are obviously in love, walk up to them and say, What went right here? They'll look at you like you are crazy. It will piss them off.

The only way to tell if a thing is just or true is to administer the test of opposites.

For example, let me tell you this true story. My friend Walt, who taught at the college where Rene used to teach, was my jogging partner after I quit drinking. Five years ago his wife left him, or they left each other. Anyway, she moved out. I don't mean to make value judgments, but I don't think they were ever happy. Afterwards, Walt was seen at parties with two or three divorcees who live here in town, nice women all, and then he fell for Joanne. They were together for almost two years. One day when we were jogging he told me that she had begun seeing another man. That was the end. The next year rumor had it that Walt was going out with one of his former Philosophy students, a woman less than half his age.

He didn't mention it. But one day, after I'd fallen off the wagon, he invited me over to his apartment for a drink. Her name was Leslie, and I could see why he would go for her, although they had nothing I could see in common. They had moved in together, and he was happier than I had ever seen him. Then the next I knew she had moved out. For a couple of days, he didn't show up at the park where we jog. When I was sure he was refusing to answer his phone, I called the resident manager at the apartments, a guy Walt played bridge with, and asked him to check on Walt, to make sure he was at least eating. The guy, his name was Mickey, called me back that evening and said Walt had blown his brains out. People pondered Walt's death. He didn't leave a note. They wanted to know why. They wanted an explanation. They wanted words. What they settled on was that he just could never find himself. That he couldn't accept things as they are, whatever the hell that means.

But this is my point about the test of opposites.

Forget about Walt for a second and replace him with Terri, his former wife, and apply the test of opposites. Make everything the same, just switch Terri for Walt. You have a middle-aged woman whose husband moves out. She falls in love with a man, spends two years with him only to discover that he is seeing another woman. Poor thing, people say. Then she falls for a guy half her age. Poor, poor thing people say. Then *he* moves out. Poor pathetic thing, people say. Then when they hear that she has killed herself with sleeping pills or something, they say, that former husband of hers is the reason for this.

Administer the test of opposites. If you don't like the results, make your own test. Just make it true. That's the hard part. That's what I'm working for.

Tell me if I am wrong. Before things happen, I have the Golden Rule. After things happen, I have the test of opposites to keep me on track, to help me make sense of things. Try it sometime. Tell me if you find that people and ideas and theories keep colliding with themselves. You'll see how flimsy words can be.

Don't get me wrong. I'm all for love. It's no addiction, but it is as deep a craving as a person can feel, and to have had it and to then go without it is worse than anything. There are no twelve-steps or stick-on patches or injectable substitutes to relieve the need for love or the effects of having to live without it. I'm more in favor of it than probably anybody you know. When I pray, I pray for love, for someone to love, for someone to love me. I've seen the time I'd die for it. Really. And I hope I see that day again. I've not given up on it. And if I ever find that person again, I would say to her, I'll prove it to you. Somehow I'll prove it to you. And if that meant putting a bullet through my brain, I would do it. I swear to God I would do it for that kind of love.

When I was in the hospital once drying out, I read a book about John Lennon. A nurse named Megan, who was about my age, gave it to me. I was thankful. The book was junk reading, but it helped take my mind off things for a while. It was called *Loving John*. One part of the book described Lennon's life while he lived in Los Angeles, while he was working on the *Rock 'n' Roll* album with Phil Spector.

I don't believe an awful lot of what I read in that sort of book. You know, the writer writes dialogue as if he was there and remembers it verbatim, and tries to get into the person's head. But the writer does make reference to what I believe is a true quotation, true in meaning anyway. It is attributed to Harry Nilsson, another songwriter and Lennon's drinking pal. He said, "Everything's the opposite of what it is." And if you will take some time to hold that thought in your mind as you look around at things, I think you'll find that too often it is true. In a world where people demand visible scars or words to explain what can't be explained, it makes a hell of a lot of painful sense. So when people ask you why it didn't work out, you just say, "There's never a reason why." You tell them that. And if they look at you and say, "Why's that?" You just remember Harry and say, "Because everything is the opposite of what it is."

My friend Billy Mims—who was also introduced to me by my future-former-wife, Rene—and I are converts to the Nilsson philosophy. We have our reasons. We are true believers.

The other night we were watching the Francis Ford Coppola film

Apocalypse Now on VCR. Billy is teaching *Heart of Darkness* as a part of his film appreciation course. When the video ended, he changed the channel and we witnessed live the landing of Marines in Somalia. There were lights and camera crews and satellite dishes everywhere, and the Marines were responding admirably. We looked at one another and in one voice said, "Everything's the opposite of what it is."

Like me, Billy loves music. He prides himself on his knowledge of music trivia. He has all kinds of theories about the evolution of popular music. So that's what we talk about mostly. The only things he asked for in his divorce were the stereo and his music collection. And that's all he's going to get, according to what he says.

'He's still pretty bitter sometimes. I feel sorry for both of them. I like them both. Lana, his second wife, wanted a reason why he didn't love her, he says. But he couldn't give her one, at least not one good enough for her or her friends. She loved him, she said, which was all she or anybody else could do, all that he could ever ask for. He couldn't argue with that. If she were an awful person, she could understand that, she said. If there were another woman she could understand that, she said. But he had to tell her, she said. He couldn't just leave her like that, without a word, just leave her like a suicide without a note. She would understand, she said, but she had to have something to understand. He had to say IT. Which of course he couldn't do because there aren't words for all things. So this went on for a year. The year of the conversation, Billy calls it.

Not everything is final yet. Like I said, he's still a little bitter. So I try to keep him talking music and off marriage.

Billy says some pretty wild things sometimes, which is allowable under the Nilsson system. But sometimes he's out there on his own planet. A few days ago, we stopped at a bar called The Paradise Lounge. There was a time I knew everybody there by first name. George Miles was the bartender then. Now the drinks are cheaper, but I don't drink any more. I'm hoping to get my pharmaceutical sales job back. I'll have a club soda occasionally.

When I go to The Paradise with Billy, I see all sorts of things that I never saw when I used to practically live there. I mean I slept there, woke up there. And now I see things I never saw, people and things that have always been there. I don't know anybody there now, and nobody knows me.

Anyway, we were sitting at the bar I used to know so well.

"There was a time when it was okay for us to talk about women's issues," Billy said. I didn't know where he was going with this, but without thinking I laid my palm in the center of the stool beside me and leaned away from him. "Don't you want to hear this?" he said.

"Just saving a seat for Nilsson," I said.

"If it weren't for men like me and you, Josh, men who acknowledged the wrongs done women in the past, who, when we were in college, stood up for them, they never would have made the gains they've made."

"You know that Lennon song, 'Woman is the Nigger of the World?'" I thought that might steer him into music talk.

"*Sometime in New York City* album." He thought for a second to confirm the album title, then continued. "That's just what I'm talking about. That came out in '70."

"You told me that was the best song on the album," I said.

Billy gave me a You-are-such-a-dumb-shit look. "BB," he called to the pretty new bartender, "bring this moron another club soda. Help me sober him up." He lit a cigarette. "My point," he said leaning in, "is that in a democracy, ours anyway, you can only really change things from the inside out. Vietnam taught us that. You and I, men of our generation, we learned that. Men like you and me wanted to make things right. We really did. We really did want to make things right. For everybody."

"That's true," I said. "But go back and watch *Woodstock*. Then remember that about 70,000 of those 100,000 hippies voted for Reagan. Twice."

"You're right," Billy said. "And I just sat through an English Department meeting in which Karen said, 'Won't a woman run for this committee; I want to vote for a woman'. And Andrea said, 'I won't speak against my gender, so–' and nobody bats a goddamn eye."

"Everything is the opposite of what it is," I said, hoping to put an end to it.

"There is only one answer for women if they want to truly break the chains that bind them." He waited for me to ask the question.

"Probably not a good idea to tell women what they need," I said.

"You're right, only a woman can know. Forgive me," he said, reaching for his drink.

I really didn't want to go on with this. He lit another cigarette.

"Did I tell you that Lana and I went to Chicago on our honeymoon?"

"No, you never told me that. Let me buy the next round." I signaled BB.

"Yeah, Chicago is a great honeymoon town, shopping, hotels, greatest blues in the North, great entertainment, the best. Did I tell you we went to the *Oprah Winfrey* show?"

I didn't say anything.

"You know," he whispered, "they divide the audience in half. Outside the entrance to the studio there are signs that designate which side you're to sit on. You didn't know that, did you? On one side the sign says, 'We don't need men.' The other side says, 'Why can't men meet our needs?'

"I never miss Oprah," I said. "I am a great lover of spectacle of every sort. But I don't ever remember seeing you in the audience."

"Maybe you missed it."

"Impossible. I know them all by heart, the way some people know every line of dialogue in every *Andy Griffith Show*."

"Well you ought to remember this one, then. It was all about PMS."

"Give it a rest," I said.

"Okay, but I know what can bridge the gender gap, can free women from the oppression of ages, what would make me adored by women if only I were a woman." He finished off his drink, then picked up the fresh one when BB slid it before him. "Did I ever tell you I'm a lesbian trapped in a man's body?"

"What's the answer, Billy," I said.

He stopped, held his drink suspended before him, and looked at me for a second. Slowly, he set his drink on the bar.

"Ask any child expert, and they'll tell you that the essential social characteristics of a person are shaped by the time they are five years old." He was leaning in now, confidential and serious.

"Yeah," I say.

"So it's not men who tell them to keep their skirts down, who tell them they have to hide and save what's under there, who teach them sayings like, 'A man's not going to buy the cow when he's getting the milk for free.' Imagine. It's not the father who insists on dressing his daughter in pink frilly slips or who enrolls her in tap class. Fathers don't make their daughters into bimbo cheerleaders."

"Would you repeat the question?"

"Women," he said, "have to teach young girls to kill their mothers. It's the only answer."

Billy turned his head from side to side like it was the saddest news he'd ever heard. He reached for his cigarettes. I slid off the stool and walked away.

The mouth of the jukebox sucked in the dollar bill. I flipped the pages of CD titles. I pressed the buttons. The sharp, clear brassy sound of the orchestra at the beginning of "All You Need Is Love" suddenly blasted from the speakers. I made another selection. For an instant, I reached for the whiskey that wasn't on the jukebox, the way a smoker who gave it up twenty years ago will unconsciously bring his hand up to his shirt pocket for no apparent reason.

Billy was laughing at the top of his voice. You could see the tears. People were looking at him. "I hate you, you bastard," he shouted from across the way. He ran his sleeve across his face. "I hate you," he shouted again. I could feel the concussion of the music against my back. Then he finished it in a softer voice. "You bastard, you," he said.

Epilogue
Dance Party
Joshua Severance

The first year we were married we called each other by the name of sexual parts or acts. She was Blowjob or Tuna. She called me Hosebag. Her vagina was Lucy, my penis was Ricky. And sometimes at restaurants she'd say, What's Ricky having, and I'd say, What's on the menu for Lucy.

We bought a house in an old neighborhood in a town in South Carolina where people still wanted to live at the country club. We got it for what we'd been paying in rent. Upstairs there was a large room that we figured had once been for a live-in housekeeper. The paint was gray from time and from a chimney fire. But underneath was old white pine with a rich grain that comes from slow growing. I began sanding away the paint, and later on, when I'd nearly finished and was living alone, my friends would show up on Wednesday nights and let themselves in and come upstairs without knocking. I began calling the upstairs room The Bar None.

The only other place we'd lived was an apartment on the Texas gulf. Rene taught only in the mornings. But I wouldn't get home until late afternoon. The sun would be bright, and even after wearing sunglasses I'd have to give myself a minute for my eyes to adjust to the cool dim light inside. I'd take off my shoes and socks. The cool parquet floor soothed the soles of my feet and worked up my ankles. Sometimes I would fill a glass with ice and bourbon and sit in a low chair in the dark apartment and just look through the sliding glass doors at her beside the tall brick wall that separated us from the rest of the world. She would be lying on her stomach on a lounge chair with a towel under her. She was already Texas brown, and in the small of her back I could see two oval pools and the bright trails that led down to them. She'd be reading some Milton scholarship through hair that hung straight down and nearly covered her glasses. Her nipples just barely touched the damp towel under her. She didn't know I was watching, and sometimes she wouldn't hear the doors sliding open.

"How are things in Paradise?" I said.

She smiled up at me. "How's it hanging, Hosebag?"

"Anything new from Uncle Milton?"

"You won't believe it," she said suddenly animated. Her intelligence only made her more beautiful. She sat up, covering her breasts with her left arm. "Guess where I found this? In the Lost and Found. Can you believe it? Is that mystical, or what?" Her eyes made tiny wrinkles when she laughed. "I don't know who's teaching this edition, but it's a shitty piece of work."

Almost every evening I would cook outside on the grill and drink while she bathed and later broke cold heads of lettuce into wooden bowls. After dinner she would sometimes beg me to take her dancing. But I am no dancer.

Soon after Rene left me, some of us got up the Wednesday Night Supper Club. It's what we had in the place of other things. I don't know who named it the Wednesday Night Supper Club. I suppose one or two of the guys who didn't want their kids to know referred to it euphemistically when they said goodbye to their wives. One Christmas Eve George Miles and Rene's colleague, Billy Mims, who didn't have wives anymore, showed up wearing reindeer horns. George had a stuffed and mounted deer's head under one arm. Topping the stairs, he announced the grand opening of a new lodge, a new order he called it. The Alc's Club. Until about a week after New Year's it was the Alc's Club, but by Valentines it was again the Wednesday Night Supper Club at The Bar None.

Before Rene left me I knew something was up. I knew it for a couple of months. I kept after her about it until finally she said, "I don't love you, Josh."

"I don't understand," I said.

"Which word gives you trouble?" she said.

I came home and George's truck was backed up to the front steps. I helped him and Billy with the sofa. Rene was at her new apartment putting up our wedding china. Later the three of us sat on the steps and had a few beers. I waved at the neighbors. Billy went to the Piggly Wiggly and bought another twelve pack of beer. George and Billy and I waved at the neighbors. By the time we'd finished most of the beer, it was dark and George said they'd better go. There were no more neighbors to salute. That sofa was a bitch, he said. I offered to follow them over and give them a hand, but Billy said there was help at the other end and handed me the last beer. I went inside and sat on the floor where the sofa had been with my back against the radiator and watched TV and ate a whole bag of potato chips. I saved the beer until I was done.

There was a PBS special on the Pharaohs, and for a time I understood about them and the rational explanations for their mummification. It all made sense to me as it was being explained. And a lot of the mumbo jumbo about the pyramids was straightened out and they didn't seem quite so mysterious. When I woke up I ran my hands down the cool ribs of the radiator. I put the potato chip bag and the beer can in the trash and went to bed. But I was still so drunk I couldn't remember which side I was supposed to sleep on.

In this state, twelve is the magic number. That's the number of points the Department of Motor Vehicles allows before you lose your driving privileges. Billy Mims and George Miles and I had been playing the subtracting game for months. My lawyer, John Truett, reigning king of The Bar None, had been reduced to two wheels before the bar's first anniversary. It didn't seem to matter that he was an attorney; the Mothers Against Drunk Driving have a lot of pull in this town. I've never seen a man who could drink so much and still stay up on two wheels. Picture a circus bear on a bicycle and you'll be close.

One warm Wednesday night we heard the sound of bent spokes and fenders on the sidewalk below. John arrived with swollen, bloody knuckles. Billy slipped downstairs and phoned John's home number to make sure there was a voice at the other end. There was, and Billy hung up. John was pretty drunk. He tried to talk George into driving them to The Paradise Lounge for a little action. George said they were both too drunk. They played pool. Somehow the upstairs had gotten a pool table and two pinball machines and a real bar.

Later, John forgot that the old toilet didn't work and was about to empty his bladder when Billy reminded him. He weaved back to the pool table with his fly down. George glanced up from a straight-in shot on the nine ball, and without hesitation said, I'd be ashamed to let everybody know my old lady had a hole that big in her ass.

Then the two of them went round and round the table. John held his cue up high. He had tears in his eyes. You can't talk that way about my wife, he kept shouting. I tried to head off John, but he had that suicidal valentine look in his eye. Billy was no help. He just kept shouting, They'll turn into butter, they'll turn into butter! George made for the stairs. John tripped, did somersaults down the steps, and broke his leg. That's when he quit drinking permanently. It was a hard fall.

When you really fall in love with someone, you don't think about all the reasons why it might not work out. Or at least you shouldn't. You just have a feeling and you want to go on having that feeling and you think that you will. You count on that. You just belong together. That's all.

When Rene and I first met it was at The Peachtree Plaza in Atlanta. I thought she was another pharmaceutical salesman. I sell hospital supplies, make my money in bandages and wraps. I took a seat beside her at the bar and said, You here for the convention? She said, Yeah. We went on for a few minutes; then she said hers was the MLA convention. I read the black print on the nametag above her left breast.

"Modern Language Association?"

She looked up at me and smiled so that little wrinkles formed and said, "Malaise," then hooked her arm around mine and I ordered another round. Later she asked me to take her dancing, but we did something else. I forget what.

As it turned out, almost everything in the house belonged to Rene. When it was all moved out, the place looked twice as big. I sold the TV and bought a second-hand industrial floor buffer. Every Saturday morning I waxed the hardwood floors with good wax and buffed them until they looked like swirls of light. That way it seemed okay that there was no furniture. I sort of liked it that way.

I left messages on Rene's machine. Some were serious. I'd write out what I wanted to say and read it so that I would sound intelligent and not waste time. Once, I wrote a twenty-page letter to her. I would read until the second beep, and then call again and pick up where I left off. She didn't return my call. Then sometimes after a bourbon or two I'd be witty. I'd call, disguise my voice, and say I was a student and had a question about English. Once I said, Could you explain the difference between screeching to a grinding halt and grinding to a screeching halt? Then I laughed out loud like a fool. I couldn't help it. That didn't work either. Then once I tried being profound. After the beep I asked in a British accent, Had you rather walk to school or carry your lunch?

Sometime in early spring while I was buffing the floors, John Truett got his license back. He showed up at our house one morning with the other guys and told me he was holding a special ceremony at the bridge over Black Creek. I unplugged the buffer and wrapped the cord around the electric motor and put the buffing pad away.

It was about a mile walk, but nobody was in a hurry. There were a couple of bottles going around. John pushed the bike and formed the center of our troop. The sun was bright, and we walked in the shadow of blooming dogwoods down the long slope to the creek. The walk down was easy.

John's bike looked funny lying on its side on the bridge railing. It looked like a dead animal maybe. Certainly not like a bicycle. The wheels of time go round and round, John began. And the time to say goodbye is always the hardest. I'm glad you can all be here to share in this final goodbye. Then he lifted the bike over his head, pirouetted, and heaved it over the side of the bridge. We all applauded and then took a narrow trail down to the water's edge and sat in the shade.

The combined strength of Billy, George, and me was required to get John back up the trail. The uphill walk home was hot and over bright. Even the air seemed dull and heavy.

Back at the house I took off my shoes and socks and walked on the cool waxed floors. I walked through every empty room. Then I took off my shirt and lay on my back on the wooden floor in the living room. I looked up at the high ceiling. When I woke up it was dark outside. I'd been dreaming but I didn't know what about. I didn't know what time it was.

Finding the trail back down to the water under the bridge was easy. The moon was full and the dogwood blooms were tiny night-lights. The water was really cold and faster than you'd think, but I found the bicycle easily enough. My trousers must have held forty pounds of water and mud. I took them off and tied them to the handlebars to balance my sample case of wraps and bandages. I just wore my boxers.

Rene's apartment was at the bottom of a hill. I could see the lights upstairs from pretty far away. I put my feet up on the handlebars and leaned back. The pedals went round and round on their own. The wind rushed past my ears. I laid the bike over easily on the wet grass and went to her door. There was music inside.

Funny, when she opened the door, the whole place smelled of Rene. Maybe it was the flowers. It was her place. She was wearing her housecoat and held a finger in her book. She leaned forward and squinted into the shadows. She flicked on the porch light and looked down at the front of my boxers. I looked down at the front of my boxers.

"Big Al and the Twins would like to know if you'd like to come out and play," I said.

"I have to make a telephone call," she said, and closed the door.

I stood outside and watched the newly hatched insects form spinning moons around the porch light. After a time she opened the door again. She'd pushed her glasses up on her head. She smiled. She hooked her arm around mine. I offered her my sample case of wraps and bandages.

When I was a kid, I shared a small bedroom with my two brothers. I slept on the top bunk. At night my older brother would play the radio beside his bed. I'd lie there in the dark on my back and listen to the low music. I could lift my hand and touch the coarse ceiling. Every night we listened to Dance Party. The DJ read dedications from people as far away as Memphis and Alexandria. He'd begin with – This number goes out to–and then he'd read the names of couples who were couples at the time. Sometimes it would take him several minutes to read all of them. Or it seemed that way to me. Some of the requests would be in code, like–This song goes out to J–and the girl in fifth period study hall with special eyes.

And now when I think about those dedications, I envision some of them being written in hieroglyphics, and the DJ at home rising from his sleep and gliding his numb fingers over miles and miles of carved stone until he discovers the etched pictures that save love, there to stand forever.

Dr. Virgil conjured a flaring lighter out of his pocket so swiftly it seemed it must have been already ignited there, that he had drawn a flame out of himself, the gesture and the igniting one movement; he held the light for M. Laruelle. "Did you never go to the church for the bereaved here," he asked suddenly, "where is the Virgin for those who have nobody with?"

Over the town, in the dark tempestuous night, backwards revolved the luminous wheel.

Malcolm Lowry
Under The Volcano